AS ANGELS SING

AS ANGELS SING

LINDA BUICE

Copyright © 2017 Linda Buice.

All rights reserved. No part of this book may be used or reproduced by any means, graphic, electronic, or mechanical, including photocopying, recording, taping or by any information storage retrieval system without the written permission of the author except in the case of brief quotations embodied in critical articles and reviews.

WestBow Press books may be ordered through booksellers or by contacting:

WestBow Press
A Division of Thomas Nelson & Zondervan
1663 Liberty Drive
Bloomington, IN 47403
www.westbowpress.com
1 (866) 928-1240

Because of the dynamic nature of the Internet, any web addresses or links contained in this book may have changed since publication and may no longer be valid. The views expressed in this work are solely those of the author and do not necessarily reflect the views of the publisher, and the publisher hereby disclaims any responsibility for them.

Any people depicted in stock imagery provided by Thinkstock are models, and such images are being used for illustrative purposes only. Certain stock imagery © Thinkstock.

ISBN: 978-1-5127-8697-2 (sc)
ISBN: 978-1-5127-8696-5 (hc)
ISBN: 978-1-5127-8698-9 (e)

Library of Congress Control Number: 2017906985

Print information available on the last page.

WestBow Press rev. date: 9/1/2017

In memory of my sister, Wiffer. We miss you!

CHAPTER 1

*L*ife's unexpected turns can bring a real test of faith, especially when fear makes you doubt your decisions.

Robin glanced in her rearview mirror at Tina in the backseat. She looked so cute wearing the headphones Marcy had given her as a parting gift. She sure loved her music, and her body moved to the music as she colored on her drawing pad—so innocent and happy for now.

Robin's hands tensed as she saw the familiar highway marker. Twenty more miles until the Lima exit. The thought of moving back to her hometown to begin living with her mother after all these years filled her with anxiety and doubts.

Her phone's ring and Marcy's familiar voice coming through the speakers interrupted her thoughts. "Hey, Robin, checking in on you. I'm worried about you and Tina. Are you sure you need to live with your mom?"

"I'm having doubts already, but my dad wanted me to try to have a relationship with her again. I can't make it on my own now that Dad's gone. This job doesn't pay enough to live on my own."

"I know you need that job, but I watched your mom at your dad's funeral. She hardly spoke to you, and she sure wasn't warm and loving to Tina, either. How could she be so cold?"

"I can't talk now, Marcy. Tina might hear. I'll give you a call after we're settled. Okay?"

"Sure thing. Remember—call me anytime day or night. I'm only an hour away. I'll be praying for you two."

"Thanks. We need all the prayers we can get. Talk to you soon."

Just as Robin finished the conversation, Tina took off her headphones and asked, "Are we almost there, Momma?"

"A few more miles, sweetie." Robin looked back in the mirror. Tina smiled and returned to the drawing, which was probably for her mother. She was so loving and affectionate.

Apprehensive thoughts returned to Robin's mind. Life without Dad left a void. *I don't understand why all this is happening, God. Why did I have to lose my job too? Is this part of your plan? Why do I feel like the prodigal returning home? Wasn't it my mom who turned her back on me? Help me, please. I feel so alone.*

Robin's mind thought about the last time she felt like this. Having a Down syndrome child at the age of twenty-five had put her life in turmoil. Her husband and mother had pushed for an abortion. The decision not to abort was only supported by her father but was the right choice. *What is it you want, Lord? Haven't I forgiven them and moved on?*

Being a single mom was a challenge, but her dad had always secretly helped and supported her. He not only accepted Tina with his whole heart, but he also appreciated just how special she was and cherished the times he spent with her. Before his death from cancer, she promised him she would try to reconcile with her mom in the near future, but unexpected unemployment forced her to face the issue now.

Tina missed her "poppy" and drew pictures of him every day. Tears always ran down her face when she drew, but she never asked questions.

Lord, why are these feelings coming back?

"Tina, we're here, honey," she said as she pulled into the driveway. *Lord, give me the strength to do this. Please let her love my little girl. Help her to see her through your eyes.*

The outdoor light was on. *Your will, Lord. I know you are with me.*

Pastor Chris looked at the calendar hanging on the wall in his office and sat back in his chair. Advent, a time to celebrate God's greatest gift ever to humankind, would be here in three months. How many people would look at Jesus as a gift this year? The community was in crisis due to local job losses. Church attendance was shrinking, and they might need to consider closing because of the financial shortfalls and needed building repairs. The session needed to be made aware of these possibilities.

A miracle would be needed to keep going in the next few years. Chris knew he needed to remember to keep hope alive during difficult times. His twenty years as a pastor had been a great walk with the Lord, and the Lord always came through in his own way and timing. Twelve years ago, when he first moved here, the congregation was much bigger and more active. He knew this year's Christmas service would be splendid, no matter how many people attended or how many children participated. Worshipping God was always beautiful, no matter how simple, because he would be in their midst. Now he needed to remind his staff and session members to trust in God's faithfulness in all things.

Closing his eyes, he prayed. *Father, thank you for all the love you gave me over these past years. This congregation loves you but is struggling. Help us find a way to make a difference in this world and the lives of those around us. Our hope is in you, Lord. Give me words to lead our session during this troubling time. We need you. I'm trusting you and you alone to get us through this.*

A knock at the door startled him. "Come in."

Marilyn, the church secretary, came in. "Pastor, John just called and asked me to remind you to look at those budget cuts before the session meeting tomorrow night. This is the last meeting to talk budget until the stewardship presentation. Also, Ruth Henderson has been moved to the senior adult home because her dementia made it too difficult to stay alone anymore. Her daughter called and wondered if you could fit a visit in."

"Ruth? Oh, how hard that must be on Wendy and her family. They are so close. But how is that possible? Ruth was fine when she played at the youth concert in June."

"I know. Wendy said it happened quickly. The symptoms appeared early summer and just escalated. It's so sad. I understand Ruth is depressed. She really has been independent and loves her home. Wendy was just worried about her because she was so disoriented. The doctor said she had classic dementia symptoms and that it would only get worse. This was the only option right now."

"I'll stop in later this week and try to cheer her up. At least I can pray with her."

"She'll be happy to see you. Maybe you could bring some music CDs with you. Music has been her life."

"That's a great idea. I happen to know her favorite songs."

"Did you realize that Robin Anderson was moving back to live with her mother?"

"Actually, I didn't know that. I haven't seen Betty since the funeral, and she wasn't very talkative then. They were both so emotional, but I didn't see them interact. I did notice Robin's daughter there with a friend of the family. Something seemed off. Nate has been attending services here since I first arrived. He was always alone."

"There's a long story I'll share at another time. I have an appointment I need to go to now. Here's your mail. Anything else you need before I leave?"

"Thanks, Marilyn. I didn't mean to keep you. Have a good evening."

"See you in the morning."

He added the dates and notes to his Google calendar. Marilyn gave her heart to her work and kept everything organized and running smoothly in addition to caring deeply for the members of the congregation. He didn't know what he would do without her. She was not one to gossip and only shared information he needed to know.

The beep from his cell phone was a reminder of his meeting in the library with the youth director in thirty minutes. *Time to start talking about the Christmas program,* he thought. He reached for his Bible and looked up verses on hope and God's provision. It was best to go in there prepared to encourage Molly.

CHAPTER 2

It was 4:30, and Robin and Tina would soon be here. Filled with anxious thoughts, Betty paced and kept looking out the window. Her eyes watered as she looked at Nate's picture over the mantle. His sudden death left a hole in her heart, and the house was empty without him. Now her estranged daughter and granddaughter were coming to live with her.

Betty heard Robin's Subaru pull in the driveway and took a deep breath. *Nate, I want this to work, but how am I going to do this without you? And Tina? Will I ever be able to accept her? How?*

The door opened, and Tina came in, followed by Robin. "Hi, Mom. Smells like …" she said, going over to the pot.

"White chili. Your favorite. Is it still? I should have asked."

"Not only my favorite—Tina's too. Look, Tina, brownies too. Isn't Grandma thoughtful?"

Tina let out a giggle and gave Betty a big hug. "Thank you, Grandma."

Betty wasn't prepared to be hugged and was stunned by the word *grandma*. Her body was stiff, but Tina didn't notice. Robin did, and she gave her a quick look that Betty assumed was disappointment.

"She likes to hug. Let her know if that is a problem."

"Robin, why don't we bring your things in and get you two settled?" she said without responding to Robin's comment. "I thought you would use your old room, and the guest room would be Tina's—unless she needs to be with you. I cleaned them, but decorate any way you want to make it feel like home. The walls haven't been painted in years and probably need to be updated sometime soon."

The word *home* stuck in Robin's mind as she headed to the door to bring in some things. She had never intended to live here again and wondered if this could really feel like home. Robin looked around. Betty had updated some drapes and changed some decorations, but it basically looked the same as she remembered. After the funeral, a small reception was held at the nearby Presbyterian Church, where her father had been a member. Robin and Tina had left immediately after the reception without stopping by the house because a storm was coming.

"Mom, would you mind if Tina just watched TV while I bring in a few boxes we need for tonight? Marcy and her husband will be bringing the rest of our stuff this weekend. Is there room in the garage?"

"Yes, and there's also plenty of storage space in the basement. Wouldn't you like help with the boxes?"

"No, I need help getting Tina settled while I unload. I don't want to leave her alone, and handling boxes is too much for her. She's adjusting to moving here, so I want her to have her favorite things in her room tonight. She misses her friends already."

Friends, Betty thought. "I can help her with the TV. What do you say, Tina? Shall we find a program for you?"

Tina nodded her head and smiled. Betty was amazed at how well Tina listened to her. She led her into the family room, and Tina immediately went over to the same picture of Nate she had looked at earlier.

"Poppy," she said, pointing to the picture with a tear running down her face.

Betty didn't know why she would recognize him. They hadn't known each other. Robin probably had pictures around the house. Yes, that would explain it. Or would it?

"Yes, that's ... your poppy."

Tina didn't move for what seemed the longest time.

"Let me turn on the TV and find something for you," Betty said, realizing she wasn't sure what would be appropriate for children. She flipped the channels until Tina pointed to a program she wanted.

Tina sat quietly on the couch as Betty sat in her lounge chair. Betty studied Tina's facial features and expressions as she watched the program. Her eyes had a slant to them and her head was small, but she didn't appear that different. Betty wondered if this was typical behavior for her.

Robin passed through occasionally with boxes. Betty and Tina continued to sit there with the only sound coming from the TV until Robin came in.

"I'm starving. Can we eat, Mom?"

"Dinner is ready when you are. Does Tina need to wash up before dinner, Robin?"

"Yes, I'll take her upstairs, and we'll be down in five minutes."

Betty went to the kitchen to ready the table. The anticipation of the three of them eating together filled her with apprehension. Maybe they could do this without talking about the last ten years? Was that even possible? How do you act around a child you don't know or understand? Thinking back to the hug, Betty wondered if she would ever hug back. What if she never could? Would Robin leave again and never come back? Her daunting thoughts were interrupted when Tina and Robin came into the kitchen.

Robin prepared a plate for Tina, and when everyone sat down, Robin looked at Tina. "Tina, would you like to say grace?"

"Sure," she said and reached for their hands. They bowed their heads. Tina's voice had a soft tone, and her prayer was simple. They made small talk throughout dinner. Robin had to admit her mom had made an effort with the food even though the conversation was strained and was mainly news about town. Robin noticed Tina was not her talkative self and was content to listen. Did she sense her grandmother was awkward around her?

"Mom, Tina and I will clean up. Why don't you relax?"

"No, you had a long day. Let me."

"We've got it. Tina's used to cleaning up. Aren't you, sweetie?"

Tina nodded her head again.

"Give her time, Mom. She isn't comfortable here yet and will talk more when she is."

"We'll all help. Things will go quicker, and I can help put things away."

They worked quietly, and Robin gently instructed Tina on how to do things.

"There, we're all done. Tina, say good night to Grandma."

Tina responded, "Good night. Love you." This time she hesitated, as if she wanted to hug her, but she didn't.

"Good night," was all Betty could say.

Betty sat in her chair once again while Robin took Tina upstairs. This was the first time she wasn't alone in the house since Nate died. It was such a good feeling even though things were a little tense. The laughter coming from upstairs was good to hear too. So far Tina hadn't been what Betty had expected—not like … No, she wasn't going to think about those memories. No one knew why she had been against Robin having Tina. Time would tell Tina's true nature and if her fears were founded.

"Mom," Robin called as she came down the stairs. "She was really tired and fell asleep before I finished her story. Thanks for dinner and letting us stay here. I know this isn't easy for you and that Dad's sickness and death were hard. We are all grieving here, so let's just take one day at a time. You'll need to be able to communicate how we can help around here and what you expect."

"I promised him I would try. I'm not sure how to … I mean, I don't know how to …"

"Mom, we can't see the future, but I'm trusting God in all this. He will lead the way."

"I stopped believing in God a long time ago, but tonight isn't a good time to talk about that."

"You're right. Let's just relax and pick something on TV. It's been a tiring day. We'll need to talk about Tina and her needs at some point though. Moving is something she doesn't understand. She needs hugs."

Betty didn't respond again and flipped the channel to the Hallmark channel. They sat in silence. Robin couldn't understand why she might never be able to love or hug her granddaughter. One day at a time. Maybe they could just live together without hugs. After all, Tina always knew she was loved.

Chris entered the library, and the worried look on Molly's face was noticeable.

"Hello, Chris. Sorry to call this meeting on such short notice, but we there's only a little more than two months until Christmas and I'm concerned about our Christmas program. Two young families with active, talented children stopped attending due to unemployment and family issues. Jobs are tight around here, and they may be leaving the area. I'm afraid there aren't enough children to do a big program for the Christmas service," she said.

"Molly, it's true the congregation is struggling this year and participation might change our program size, but perhaps we could think of ways to make it simpler?"

"What do you mean by simple?" she asked.

"Possibly a smaller program with fewer props and participants?"

Molly sat in silence for a moment and then asked, "You don't think people will be disappointed?"

"My experience as a pastor has shown me when kids are involved, people really don't need fancy. Sharing the Christmas message the best way we can is the important thing."

Again, there was a pause. "I can simplify. It will take some thought and creativity. Where will we find the children we need though?"

"God will supply what or who we need. Trust him. God knows your love for your ministry and all the love and effort you put into it. Let his faithfulness in the past be a reminder in the days ahead. Some older members would help if asked. In fact, they would be delighted. Sometimes I think we don't fully use their talents. We'll all need to be fervent in prayer, won't we?" he said. "Let's take it to him now." They both bowed their heads.

"Father, thank you for Molly and her dedication to this church. Help us to find a way to bring glory to your name this Christmas Eve by providing us with the children we need for our program and spirited people who will worship you the way that you so deserve. Guide us as we plan, and give us wisdom in all we do. Amen."

Chris looked up at Molly and could tell she was still nervous. "Molly, keep praying and answers will come. Please keep me posted and let me know how I may be of assistance. Kristen, Chloe, and Robbie are always willing to help. Marilyn has contact with members and can be very persuasive." He smiled at her and headed for the door.

"Simple. Hmm." Molly was talking to herself.

About an hour later, Chris sat in his office mulling over the budget. His eyes glanced out the window, and he watched Molly leaving for the day with a large box in her hands. After looking at the budget, he realized Molly wasn't the only one who needed encouragement. The budget report made the future look bleak for the church.

Lord, we need your help!

CHAPTER 3

The budget kept Chris's mind off his destination until he arrived. The Limestone Adult Home took great care of the residents, but it wasn't always a happy place. There were so many frail, forgotten adults in the last stage of life at the home. The majority of residents had been placed in the facility because their families were no longer able to care for them. Sadly, visitations from family members and friends dwindled after the first few months because visits were so depressing. The residents missed their homes, and their loss often contributed to deteriorating health. Both residents and visitors knew that the home was their final destination.

Chris thought to himself, *How did all those people in the Bible live to be over one hundred years old? Only you could do that Lord!*

As he approached the receptionist desk, he noticed a new face behind the desk. She couldn't be more than thirty-five years old, which was odd. Most young people didn't take jobs at places like this, but she looked familiar.

"Good afternoon. I'm Pastor Chris from Limestone Presbyterian Church. Do I know you?"

"Pastor Chris, I'm Robin Anderson. We met at my father's funeral—Nate Johnson—a few months back."

"Robin, sorry, I didn't recognize you. How are things with you?"

"Things have been a little rough since I lost my dad. I moved in with my mom and am trying to adjust. We're both grieving, and we haven't had a relationship since before my daughter's birth. I'm taking it one day at a time."

Chris stood there trying to take it all in. That was a lot for a young person to handle.

"Your daughter never had a relationship with her grandmother?" he asked.

"No, she didn't, and that was Mom's choice. Dad's last wish was for us to work out our differences. But you didn't come here to talk about me. How can I help you?"

"I'm actually here to see Ruth Henderson, who was just moved here. Could you please tell me what room she's in?"

"Sure, let me see." Her eyes looked to her computer screen as she continued. "It might take me a minute. I just started this week, and I'm still figuring things out."

"I'm not in a hurry."

"Here it is. Room 220B down in the dementia wing. Hit the red buzzer outside the double doors. You probably already know that," she said.

"I'm afraid I do. Several members have been here over the years. Before I go, I vaguely remember your mom. She used to be in the choir, didn't she? Someone at the funeral mentioned that, but I haven't seen her at church in a long time," he said.

"Mom and Dad loved to sing in the choir. My whole family loved the music at Sunday worship. Circumstances caused her to lose her faith in God's goodness, and she stopped going to church completely. Dad never lost his faith in God."

"Your father was a fine Christian. And how about your faith? Did you lose yours?"

"Never. My faith helped me get through all the curveballs I've been thrown by life so far. My choice to keep my baby was right for me even if my life has been complicated because of it. I don't have any regrets."

"Glad to hear. It's when we're in the valleys that we need faith the most. If you ever need to talk or need help, please give me a call."

"Actually, I'm thinking of joining church again. Dad wanted me go back to his church. Tina too."

Oh, Lord, is this an answer to our prayer?

"You would be a welcome addition. Stop by the office soon, and we can talk. Let Marilyn, my secretary, know when a convenient time would be. I can have my wife, Kristen, come over with the kids, and they can occupy Tina while we talk. Have a great day, Robin."

A peace came over Chris as he headed down the hallway. He took out his cell phone and added a quick note to ask Marilyn more about Betty Johnson.

Ruth Henderson was sitting in a chair by her window as he entered the room. She had always been a vibrant, active church member, and it was disheartening to see her here.

"Hello, Ruth," he said as he gently knocked so he wouldn't startle her. "How are you doing?"

She turned her head to speak, and he saw a single tear running down her face. "I can't say I'm fine. God has picked a new place for me, and I'm afraid I don't like it. I know I should be grateful for my life, but this doesn't feel like a place I was meant to be in."

Chris paused because he was at a loss for words. "But you're settling in?"

She looked at him questioningly.

"I noticed your Bible handy and a pile of books."

"Wendy brought them over today."

"Is there anything else you need?" he asked.

"Please pray for me and pray for God's plan for me here. One day I'll see how all the pieces of my life will fit together, but …" She choked up and was unable to speak.

"Ruth, you are on the prayer chain, and prayer is powerful. I haven't talked to your family this week, but I know your safety and well-being are what is important to them. They love you and were concerned about you." When she didn't respond, he added, "What can be done to help make you more comfortable here?"

Ruth picked up a little angel figurine from her nightstand and looked at it pensively. "Don't forget I'm here, please. You can pray that I will hear the angel's voice while I still can." She couldn't finish.

Chris noticed she was still struggling to maintain control. *What a* horrible disease, he thought. *People trapped inside seemly healthy bodies, unable to communicate.* Ruth was an educated woman. She would understand what was ahead. What did she mean by the angel's voice?

"I'll come back soon, Ruth, and the deacons plan on visiting regularly. I know there are opportunities to join in activities here too. You're not alone."

"Thank you for stopping by," she said, still holding the figurine.

Robin was doing paperwork at her desk as Chris approached.

"Have a great day, Pastor!"

"I look forward to talking with you soon."

Chris's mind switched from Ruth to thoughts about Robin and her daughter. She seemed like such a sweet person. He had a good feeling about her. The church needed new people, and Robin's testimony about the power of God's sustaining love through trials and difficulties was a message the congregation needed to embrace.

Tuesday was an unusually busy day for Chris. Getting ready for the session meeting meant preparing for the unpleasant topic of budget shortfalls. In addition to building maintenance costs going up, the church desperately needed a new roof. The economy had affected the spirit of stewardship. Higher job losses in the area over the last year accounted for lower contributions from members. The local economy always predicted pledging. The congregation needed a revival of both faith and spirit.

The opening prayer was followed by committee reports, which brought further concern and discouragement. Molly's youth ministry report brought up the Christmas Eve problems and the possibility of only having music or just a simple program. She did her best to be optimistic about the possibilities. Chris could feel their dampened spirits.

Luckily, Elder Rena spoke up. "In the fifty years of my membership here, we've always had a program, no matter how big or small. God always came through in tough times. This year won't be different, provided we don't lose our faith. He will equip us with the right people and program."

The other session members looked at her with uncertainty and shook their heads without comment.

John Larsen's budget report was last item on the agenda because time was needed to go over each line entry, and comments could be generated.

He set the tone with recommendations from his finance committee. "Membership here is declining like it is at other churches in the area. Pledges to date are down 25 percent due to the layoffs at the canning factory, and we recommend each committee should see if they can decrease spending by the same amount."

His statement produced an expected audible groan from those present.

He continued, "On top of all this, we need a new roof. The estimated cost is ten thousand dollars. If we don't fix it, there won't be a church to worry about. We don't know how we can afford a large expense at this time. My recommendation is to hold a special congregational meeting to discuss this."

Chris saw the hopelessness on their faces. He responded quickly, "Thank you for the hours your group has spent preparing this report and being good stewards with our money. It is times like this that we need to be strong in faith in our Father. So let's take what we have discussed here tonight to the Lord in prayer."

Chris began the prayer as usual and asked others to feel free to pray after him. Session members poured their hearts out to God with such abandonment and sincerity, and all the members were filled with emotion at the conclusion when they realized more than thirty minutes had passed. The prayers included thanksgiving for God's never-ending love, for a revival in their church, and for the individual urgent needs of the committees. The hopelessness of the congregation had been lifted up to the Lord.

The room emptied in silence. Chris sat alone thinking about what had transpired and the strong presence of Holy Spirit felt by all. He knew without question something *big* was about to happen. Thoughts of Robin and Tina came to mind. He couldn't help feeling they would be part of the plan. God had a way of using ordinary people to do big things. Time would reveal God's purpose, and it would probably be different from anything he could imagine. Struggle might make things difficult for a while, but in his experience, the best gifts came through pain. The better question was how much?

CHAPTER 4

*B*etty panicked when she noticed that the kitchen clock neared 3:30 p.m., which signaled time for Tina's bus to drop her off. She felt a twinge in her stomach. This was the first time they would be alone since they had moved in over a month ago. So many negative thoughts were going through her mind. *I can't care for Tina. This is too much. This isn't fair of Robin to think I should make more of an attempt to get to know Tina. Things were fine with the after-school program.*

The bus could easily be seen from the side kitchen porch window. It pulled up at the end of the driveway, and she saw Tina wave to the bus driver. The monitor waited in the doorway, watching. Tina was trying to skip but hadn't quite mastered it. She came down the driveway to the back porch and up the steps.

"Hi, Grandma," she said, smiling when she entered the kitchen.

Betty was about to tell her where to put her coat and shoes, but she got everything in the right spot without prompting. She set her backpack on the chair and took out some papers. One was a picture she had drawn, which she handed to her grandmother.

It was a simple picture of flowers and a blue sky. "It's for you," she said again, holding it out.

When there was not a response, she just put it in her backpack and waited quietly.

"Would you like a drink or a snack? Does Momma let you eat, or should you wait for her?"

Tina looked at the picture and then back at Betty. Although her smile was gone, she didn't respond.

Finally she said, "Milk, please."

Betty filled the glass, and Tina sat at the table. The phone was a pleasant interruption they both needed.

"Yes, she got off the bus okay. Did you want her to have a snack?"

Robin explained the snack routine and added, "Mom, I'll be home at five to help with dinner. Tina can listen to her music or watch TV if that's okay. Whatever is easier for you. Is everything okay?"

A little over an hour. "Things are fine, but you will be here right at five, won't you?"

Robin could sense the anxiety in her voice. "Mom, remember, we talked. We need to act more like a family and not just strangers. Give her a chance."

"We'll manage until five," she said, hanging the phone up.

Manage—manage what? This is awkward. Sure, some of my friends do take care of their grandkids full time, but they are normal kids. Why can't Robin see that?

With a big sigh she asked, "Music or TV?"

"TV."

The familiar sound of Robin's car pulling in the driveway broke their uncommunicative state. Tina ran to greet her at the door.

"I missed you, Momma."

"Me too, pumpkin. How was school?"

Betty just listened to the loving exchange, and it reminded her of Robin's childhood. Afternoons together after school had been wonderful. Robin looked at Betty. "Everything go okay, Mom?"

"No problems. Let's get dinner started."

Tina went back to the family room until Robin called her to set the table.

Tina and Robin followed a daily routine, which surprised her. Robin had done a good job, and they seemed like a typical family in that regard. And to think—she did it alone.

Although evenings were quiet, life went along. Robin made an effort to have conversations about work and things she noticed in town. Tina shared school stories each night, but Betty only half listened, denying herself the opportunity to build relationships. Her thoughts were always the same. *This will end the same way. I can't do it!*

Shortly after dinner, Robin took Tina upstairs to get ready for bed. Betty settled into her chair and waited for Robin's return which took much longer than usual. Tina didn't come down to say good night.

Robin came down the stairs with Tina's drawing in her hand. Betty could see her lips pressed together and pain in her eyes.

"Really, Mom? It's a picture. You know how much she loves to draw, and she made this for you because she was thinking about you today. All she could talk about this morning was coming right home on the bus and being with you. How could you not take it?"

"It didn't ..."

"Didn't occur to you she has feelings? She loves to draw. You won't let her hug you, so she draws pictures for you. It took me all this time to convince her that she didn't do something wrong."

"I'm sorry."

"You need to tell her that!" she said and went upstairs.

Betty sat alone with the TV blaring and recognized the same empty feeling she had experienced after Nate's death. Tears ran down her cheeks, but she didn't move from the chair.

Things were very quiet the next morning. Robin didn't want her anger to show. Despite everything going on, she was struggling to forgive. Last night she prayed for over an hour after Tina fell asleep. She cried out to God to help rid herself of the resentment building inside. While she was grateful she had a job and a roof over their heads, she didn't appreciate her mother being so cold to her innocent daughter. Circumstances had forced these living arrangements but would not dictate what she could endure.

"Tina, remember what I said last night. I'm bringing your drawing to a friend where I work. She's so sad and needs cheering up."

The smell of coffee wafted up the stairs. It was a familiar reminder of Betty's presence in the kitchen. With a deep breath, she picked up Tina's bag, and they went down to breakfast. Absent from their usual routine was conversation. No one spoke, and the silence ended when Betty answered the phone.

"Marge, I'm glad you called. I wondered if you wanted to have lunch this week."

"Absolutely. With the holiday approaching, we need to do some planning."

Robin took that opportunity to slip out with Tina before they said goodbye.

Betty finished her conversation and hung up. Shame overcame her as she watched them pull out of the driveway.

CHAPTER 5

Betty walked into the cafe and found Marge at a back table. Two coffees were already present.

"Marge, thank you for meeting me. I needed to talk to someone, and you're the only one I trust."

"Betty, we've been friends since childhood. I'm here for you. I know we planned on lunch, but I want to find on what's going on with Robin and Tina."

"Did Robin call you?" Betty asked.

"No, she didn't. I could tell from your voice that something's wrong. I'm here to listen."

Betty didn't speak for a few minutes and finally started, "Robin expects too much from me. I can't get used to having Tina around after school."

"Is she difficult to handle?" Marge asked.

"She makes all these pictures and expects me to take them and put them up."

"Most kids do that. She's obviously trying to please you."

"I'm just not used to kids."

"Look, Betty, I think you're still thinking about your cousin. As your friend, I would advise you to start caring for your granddaughter. You and Robin have lost ten years. Robin isn't going to understand your treatment of her daughter. I don't."

"You're taking her side?"

"Betty, do you understand you have a chance to have a wonderful experience with a granddaughter? I have seen Tina and Robin around town, and I would feel lucky to have Tina for a granddaughter."

Betty didn't respond.

"I didn't want to tell you on the phone, but Henry and I are leaving for Florida tomorrow. He suddenly sprung it on me. We've talked about spending winters there for some time now. You will be able to call me, but I won't be here for support. I hope you work this out with Robin before it goes too far. Nate would not be pleased."

"I'm not sure I can."

"Then I think you're making a huge mistake."

"Tell me about your Florida plans," Betty said, changing the subject.

Marge shook her head in disbelief but gave up trying to persuade Betty to change her ways.

A few days had passed since the session meeting, and no answers had come. The desk calendar was a reminder of the rapidly approaching Advent season. How many people would really feel happy during this holiday season? Christmas was often a time of pressure and stress for many families. What about all the families affected by the layoffs? For others, it could be a time of depression or loneliness. This would be the first Christmas Betty would be without her husband. Ruth would not be in her home this year. Chris was more cognizant of his members needing upbeat sermons each Sunday in December, and it wasn't too early to get started. A knock on his door interrupted his thoughts.

Through the window on his door, he saw Molly, and he motioned for her to come in.

"Chris, I wondered if you had a moment?" she asked.

"Sure, what's on your mind?" he asked.

"I just wanted to tell you how touched I was by the prayer at the end of the session meeting. By the end of our prayers, I was overcome by such a feeling of peace about our upcoming program. To be honest, for some reason my mind wandered off to the scene where the angels sang about 'all is calm' in the fields, and I haven't been able to think any other thoughts all week. What do you think it means?" she asked.

"I'm not quite sure, but I'm certain it will be revealed soon. Keep praying. Answers will come," he said.

"Thanks—I'm thinking *angels* for Christmas, but with a fresh approach. I'll decide soon, and it will be simple but memorable."

"Thanks for sharing, Molly! I needed to hear good news."

The angel talk made Chris think of Ruth's comment when he had visited her. He needed to see her again and ask her to clarify what she had said about angels. He had a reminder on his cell to ask Marilyn about Betty Johnson. The sermon notes would need to be put off, but he couldn't wait too long. Time had a way of slipping away when he was faced with so many issues.

Marilyn was busy typing the bulletin when he entered her office.

"Hello, Chris. Do you need anything?" she asked.

"I'll be heading over to the adult home to visit Ruth again later. I promised her I wouldn't forget about her. Robin Anderson is the receptionist there now. Her mother is Betty Johnson. When we held Nate's funeral a few months ago, I didn't have an opportunity to talk to her. I sensed tension between them. What can tell me about their background?" he asked.

"Chris, I don't gossip, so I can only give you the facts. Nate was actually the one who came in and poured out the sad story. He couldn't find anyone to confide in. What a heartbreaker there. Robin moved away about fifteen years ago when she went to college. She met her husband while in college, and they fell in love. They married right after graduation." She paused. "Things came apart when she became pregnant."

"You said pregnant? Why would a married couple have an issue with that?" he asked.

"They both were offered jobs in Rochester after graduation and decided to live out in the suburbs. Robin found out she was pregnant a year later, and prenatal testing showed something was not right with her unborn child. I'm not sure why she had the test. Her husband and mother wanted her to abort the baby. Both agreed a special needs child would tie them down and limit future job possibilities. I don't know the whole story, but Robin chose to keep the child. Betty got very angry at Robin—and at God. She stopped coming to church, even though Nate still attended services. He asked me to pray for his family because Betty and Robin never repaired the relationship," she finished, shaking her head.

"That must have happened when I first came here," he pondered. "God gets blamed for so many things. How is Betty with her granddaughter now?"

"I'm not sure," she answered. "Even though circumstances have forced them to live together, how do you repair such a long estrangement?"

"The Bible is full of sorrowful stories. God has a way of redeeming people and circumstances. Robin is a very pleasant young lady and seems to be coping."

"Like I said, I really don't gossip. Many of your sermons have said forgiveness is one of the hardest things to give. Betty has not come back to church yet."

"Marilyn, let's keep them on our private prayer list. Anything is possible with God. You and I will pray together at our weekly prayer time. Robin did mention she was going to schedule a meeting soon. When she does, would you please call Kristen and let her know? She can watch Robin's daughter while we meet."

"It's been years since I've seen Robin. I wonder if she'll remember me," Marilyn said.

"It won't be long until you find out."

A truck pulled in to the church parking lot. It belonged to a roofing contractor.

"I'm leaving, Marilyn. When they finish inspecting and making assessments, you can give John a call."

"I will. Tell Ruth I said hello."

"I will," he responded.

CHAPTER 6

Robin arrived promptly at four thirty. Marilyn had arranged for Kristen and the children to take Tina in the church hall until five o'clock. Apparently, Tina was familiar with Chloe and Robbie because they attended the same school.

"Have a seat, Robin. I'm glad you came in. What's on your mind?" Chris asked.

Robin hesitated and then started. "Pastor, I don't know where to start."

"You're aware that your father came to this church on a regular basis, aren't you?" he asked.

"Dad did tell me he continued to worship without Mom."

"To be honest, your father did not divulge information about your family to me. He was always alone in worship and really wasn't involved in church activities. I did know he worked in sales and traveled frequently."

"Let me give you more details. A year after I married Jeff Anderson, I found out I was expecting. Jeff and I were ecstatic. A few months into my pregnancy, due to some medical issues, my doctor did a screening. She said the test indicated I had a good chance of having a child with special needs, including Down syndrome. Jeff and my mother were very upset."

"And your dad?"

"My dad supported me and whatever decision I made."

"Meaning?"

"My husband and mother asked me to have an abortion. The idea of a special needs child was inconceivable. They did not want to read literature about it or even discuss it with professionals. Mom and Jeff had a dream about what my family should look like and didn't accept or even listen to what I wanted."

"You obviously didn't have an abortion."

"I don't believe in them. My parents brought me up in this church, and I knew life and children are gifts from a loving God. My husband did not share my decision and left me. He never contacted me again," she said with great sadness in her voice.

"What about your mother and father?" Chris asked.

"My father's traveling sales job made it easy for him to secretly be a part of Tina's life from the very beginning. His death took a piece of our life away, and we miss him. My mom had no part of anything."

"You never attempted to reconcile with her?" he asked.

"She refused to talk about it and stopped accepting my calls. My father wasn't able to reach her either. We both gave up. I had a hard time juggling being a single parent and keeping a job."

"Children do keep life busy. After ten years of not speaking, what made you decide to live with her?"

"When Dad got sick, his deathbed wish was that we would reconcile. We both agreed. My employer had to make cuts and my job was eliminated, but they had an opening in this area. I'm a social worker and work for the state, which funds the adult home here. The receptionist job keeps me in the system and available for any future opportunities. My situation forced me to ask Mom if we could live with her. This job is at a lower pay grade, but I really need to keep my health insurance."

"How are things going?"

"Even though we have lived with Mom for over a month, our relationship is superficial. She's still mad at God, hasn't accepted Tina, and pretends the last ten years never happened. Her cold treatment of Tina is intolerable, and I will move when I am in a better financial situation. Mom is afraid to love her own granddaughter," she said.

"Your situation is challenging," he responded.

"Mom's grieving for Dad, but I am too. I feel like I'll be dishonoring his wishes if we move. Dad was my rock. I know Tina is different, but she is such a blessing. I wish Mom would open up to her. We've prayed about it all this time," she added.

"God's timing is not always on our schedule, though his ways are always perfect."

"God has been good to me, but I have to admit I'm struggling with doubt right now. Why have so many bad things happened to me? Why did he have to take Dad from us?"

Questioning God was something all Christians did at times in their faith journey, but he also sensed resentment in her words.

"Robin, God loves you, he is with you, and his plan is always better. It may take time to see the whole picture. Let me ask another hard question. Have you forgiven your mother?"

"With help from Dad, I thought I had. Each day I had to get up and make an effort to forgive, and eventually I stopped thinking about her. Being back here in the same house has caused some unpleasant memories and feelings to resurface."

"True forgiveness does take daily effort. I don't have the answers, but I can pray with you about it. Okay?" he asked.

She nodded, and together they prayed that her mother might open her heart to both Tina and God.

Kristen and the kids knocked on the door. It was time to go home for dinner.

Chris watched them go down the hallway. He wished he could do more but knew God had his own way of doing things.

"Such a sweet little girl," Kristen said.

"The road they have traveled has been rough, but unfortunately they are still in the valley. There is a test of faith going on here."

Chris did not explain because the children were present and he kept meetings confidential. In his mind he was thinking Robin's pride might be a factor in this scenario.

Oddly, Robin wasn't at her desk when Chris entered the lobby of the adult home. In the lobby, a young child stood decorating a Christmas tree while humming a Christmas song. Thanksgiving was a few days away, and the staff always extended the holiday season, hoping to liven up residents.

"Hello, young lady," he said from a distance so as not to startle her.

She turned and said, "Hi, my name is Tina. What's your name?"

"My name is Chris. You came to the church with your mom a week ago. Are you in charge?" he asked.

Letting out a giggle, she said, "No, my mom—she'll be back. Wanna help?"

"Sure," he answered as she pointed to the box of ornaments.

Robin walked up before he started.

"Hi, Pastor. Sorry, we are short-staffed today, and I needed to run something down the hall. I see my little angel is entertaining you," she said with a big smile. "Decorating is her favorite thing to do. This place needed a little cheer."

"It sure does. I heard her humming while she decorated. She likes music?" he asked.

"Actually, she sings really well. Her earphones and her iPod are usually not far away. We left them home today so they wouldn't get lost."

"I'm here to visit Ruth again. How are things going at home?" he asked.

"We're still settling in and adjusting. The life we left in Rochester worked for the two of us."

"New job, new school, new home. That's a lot to handle on top of losing your dad. Tina looks happy."

"Her temperament is upbeat most of the time, but I know things are not ideal. Things are strained. I'm trusting God on this, Pastor."

"Call me Chris, please. Everyone does. Let's schedule another meeting soon."

"I need to do that."

"I guess I'd better visit Ruth now," he said, turning toward the dementia wing.

Although Ruth was in the chair by the window, the blinds were closed. The food tray on the nearby table was half eaten. She looked away when he entered, and he wondered if she even recognized him.

Before he could speak, a little voice spoke from behind him.

"Dropped 'im," Tina said as she came in with his gloves in hand. Apparently the staff had let her in.

"My angel," Ruth said, looking at Tina.

Chris looked at Ruth and the huge smile on her face. He recalled that she had asked to hear an angel's voice the first time he had visited.

"Can you sing for me, my little angel?" Ruth asked.

Tina looked to Chris for permission. Robin entered the room before he answered.

"Sorry, she took off too quickly. Everyone knows her here and probably saw the gloves and let her in. I'm sorry; it won't happen again," Robin said.

"Sing, my little angel," Ruth said with urgency.

Her plea stunned them all. As far as Robin knew, Tina had never sung here.

Tina looked at her mom for approval, and she nodded.

Tina moved next to Ruth and began to sing, "Shine, Jesus, Shine."

Chris couldn't believe what he was hearing. Such a soft, angelic voice—how? Tina appeared to have a speech impediment, but when she sang, it was not noticeable. This was truly a gift from God.

"I don't think I've seen Ruth this happy since she arrived," a nurse said from behind. "You, my dear, will need to come back and sing again."

Robin said, "That's a possibility. She loves music and singing. I'm sorry, but I need to get back. Could we talk on the way? Annie is covering the desk."

Mary, who was the floor nurse, walked out with them.

Chris stayed and visited with Ruth. That song had definitely uplifted her spirit and had left her in a better mood. Music was her life passion, and she had taught it in the elementary school for over thirty years. Mary, Robin, and Tina were sitting in the lobby talking when Chris went to sign out.

"How about Sunday afternoon, December 4? Can you come back and sing? Is it a date?" she asked, looking at Robin. They both nodded.

"Chris, Mary wants Tina to come back to sing for the residents—doesn't she, sweetie?"

Tina proudly nodded her head.

"You, little lady, made Ruth very happy. I'm certain other residents would love to have you sing for them." His comment made Tina giggle.

"I knew she could sing. I just didn't think much about doing it for the residents. Mary does her best to plan activities to cheer them up. Having children sing hasn't been one of them."

"It's worth a try. Ruth perked right up when Tina sang."

Mary was truly delighted with Tina.

"Robin, I look forward to seeing you soon. And you too, Tina."

They exchanged goodbyes, and Tina, Robin, and Mary went back to planning.

Chris spent the rest of his walk to the car thinking about what had just transpired, and his mood was crushed when he got a text message from John stating that the roof estimate exceeded expectations.

Lord, please help us find a way to meet our needs. Advent is a week away, and we need to lift the spirits at your church.

CHAPTER 7

The Sunday Advent service was poorly attended. The sanctuary was decorated for Christmas with candles in the windows and lighted garlands around the sides of the pews. The Advent candle was ready to light, and the large manger scene was set up next to a Christmas tree. It looked beautiful. Advent signified the preparation for Christ's birth and the anticipation of his return. Although he understood the difficulties families were facing, he was disappointed at the attendance.

When he stepped up to the pulpit to deliver his sermon, he noticed two people come in and sit in the back. It was Robin and Tina. Tina waved as she moved into the pew with her mother. His sermon focused on God's great love for his children.

He concluded by saying, "God made you and loves you. He has plans for your life—every detail of it. Each of you was made for a specific purpose, and each of you is special. When you view the cross and see Jesus's arms stretched out, remember how much you are loved." Chris watched Tina as he spoke and saw her eyes were focused on the crucifix.

When the closing hymn started, he could hear the little angel voice coming from the back of the sanctuary. Molly and John immediately turned to see where the voice was coming from. Their faces revealed amazement, and Chris knew exactly what they were thinking.

Standing at the exit at the conclusion of the service, Chris shook hands with people exiting to go to the fellowship hall. He did not see Robin or Tina but found them waiting outside his office.

"Hello," Tina said, bubbly. "I'm singing today."

"I know—I can't wait," he replied. "I'm coming to listen, and I'm bringing my family."

Marilyn came down the hallway, bringing the collection money to the office. "You must be Tina," she said.

"I wondered, do you have a moment?" Robin asked.

"Tina, would you like to help me find some cookies in the fellowship hall?" Marilyn asked.

"Okay, Momma?" Tina asked.

"Sure, just don't eat them all," Robin answered. "She loves cookies."

Chris took the collection plate and opened his office door. "Come on in, and have a seat. What's on your mind?" Chris asked.

Robin hesitated and then started. "I feel awful coming to you again and taking up your time."

"Not a problem. I'm always available. You look troubled. Did something happen?" he asked.

"You know Tina's singing today?"

"Yes, my whole family's looking forward to it. Are you changing your mind?"

"No, Tina loves to sing, and I've seen what it did for Ruth. I hoped my mother would attend, but she responded negatively to our invitation."

"What did she say?"

"Mom used to sing in the church choir. Her voice is beautiful, and she sang in the choral society too. She's never heard Tina sing and asked me why I would want to embarrass myself by letting her sing in public."

"Doesn't Tina sing around the house?"

"No. We sing in her room every night before she goes to sleep but not around Mom. She can sense Mom wants to keep her at a distance because Mom only speaks to me about her and in a general way."

Chris could hear pain in her trembling voice. "Does your mom still keep you at a distance?"

"Chris, I'm struggling with her. We all live in the same house and tolerate each other, but we have a real disconnect. We're not a family. Luckily, Marcy and her husband came down for Thanksgiving and stayed in town overnight. This is the first holiday without Dad, so cooking kept us all busy. Marcy's kids were a treat for Tina. Mom only talks to me about food or events in town. She has friends she plays bridge with on Saturdays and a book club that meets on Fridays. We don't get personal and *never* talk about the past."

"This afternoon is going to be great for Tina and everyone involved. Keep your mind steady on the Lord, and be patient. He *can* change people; we can't. We need to extend grace to others, even when they don't deserve it."

"Thank you. You're right, and this afternoon will be good for Tina. We'll see you over there. Now I need to find her before she eats too many cookies."

"Marilyn makes the best Christmas cookies. I want to have a few myself."

They walked down to the fellowship hall together. Chris prayed silently on the way. *Lord, please help Betty make the right choice about this afternoon. Help Robin to find the same grace and unconditional love for Betty as you have for us. They all need each other and you.*

Sundays at the home were often solemn and depressing. For patients who were alert but not able to live alone, they felt trapped. Coupled by the fact they were unable to go to church, the mood was often somber. Most felt abandoned by their families and had nothing to look forward to in the afternoons.

Susan, the manager of the home, was delighted to hear Tina was going to sing. When Mary told her how uplifting it had been for Ruth, she wanted to see what music would do for other patients. The Christmas decorations were always put up mid-November because it changed the atmosphere.

The large open room had an unused piano in the corner. They weren't worried about anyone getting away because some of the staff had called families to come. This was an experiment to see if patients would respond favorably to Tina. Ruth's mood had improved so much since Tina's song.

At three o'clock Susan noticed only six patients in the room. Tina and Ruth were having a conversation about a picture of an angel Tina had drawn for Ruth as they waited patiently for Robin to give them the signal to begin. Robin's intentional delay meant she hoped Betty had accepted her invitation. The residents sat with family members in anticipation. Chris sat with his wife, Kristen, and children, Chloe and Robbie. Betty stood in the back of the room near the door, where she was not visible.

Robin gave Tina a hug and asked her to begin. She started singing "Jingle Bells." A hush came over everyone when she began. Though she didn't pronounce all the words correctly, she was so innocent no one cared. Her mom played soft background music for the first song on a CD player. No one expected a voice so sweet and soft. She continued by singing "Jesus Loves Me," "We Wish You a Merry Christmas," and "Rudolf, the Red-Nosed Reindeer."

Chris observed one of the family members recording the songs on their iPhone. Once the music started, it had carried down the hallways. Steadily, more patients and staff came in to listen. One elderly patient tugged on the arm of his nurse and whispered in her ear.

As Tina finished, the nurse walked over and asked if Tina would sing "Silent Night" for her patient.

"Oh, I'm sorry," Robin responded. "I don't have that song on the CD."

Ruth came over and said, "I can play the piano."

Tina didn't give anyone time to answer. She headed over to the piano with Ruth.

Ruth hadn't played the piano in a long time, and Susan wondered if she could still play. She had retired as a music teacher twenty years ago. Ruth had had fewer episodes since Tina had started visiting her. She was happy and eating again. Perhaps she could play too.

It took Ruth a few minutes to get situated, but once she started playing, Tina began to sing. The audience was in awe as they listened to her, especially an elderly gentleman who had tears in his eyes. Chris was sure the song was an important memory for him. This little girl was very special indeed. Chris glanced back at Betty, and her eyes also were brimming with tears. Perhaps the song had a significant meaning for her too.

CHAPTER 8

Monday was back to work as usual for Chris. The proposed cuts from session members were on his desk. There still wasn't a Christmas Eve program ready, but good things were happening. Yesterday at the home had been like a worship service for the residents. Chris made a note to speak to Susan about doing more activities like that for the residents.

Chris thought back to his conversation with Robin. What a sad situation for Robin and her mother. Everyone who met Tina loved her. Why didn't her grandmother? Yesterday's program had brought incredible joy to the residents and the rest of the audience. Some people choose not love as Jesus taught them to—unconditionally. It seemed like something was holding Betty back from letting herself love again.

Chris spent Monday and Tuesday in meetings and planning Advent services.

Across town, things were not going well. For two days Betty and Robin had avoided talking about Sunday. On Wednesday, Robin stopped by Tina's room as she headed down to prepare breakfast. Tina sat at her desk in her room making another picture for Ruth.

"Sweetie, I'll call you when breakfast is ready," she said.

"Okay," Tina answered as she kept coloring.

Robin's mother sat reading the paper as she walked into the kitchen.

"Mom, how about going with us to get a Christmas tree today after school?" Robin asked.

"Christmas will not be the same without your father here. Maybe we should skip the tree this year," she responded firmly.

"We miss him too, Mom, but Dad would want life to go on. Tina loves Christmas and decorating. It would be a great family activity. We would love it if you came with us," she said.

Betty paused before answering and finally responded, "No, I don't care to go, and what could *she* know about decorating? I hope you don't think you will be using the decorations in the attic."

"What does that mean? She has a name." Robin's voice rose in anger. "You haven't given her a chance. Everyone else does."

"You mean everyone else feels sorry for her, don't you?" Betty snapped back.

"Sorry for what?" Robin said sharply.

"Sorry you are burdened with a child like that! You heard her Sunday. She should be in a home or someplace. Not here." She stopped because Tina stood in the doorway.

Tina's teary eyes were a clear indication she had overheard part of the conversation. "Tina, honey, go upstairs and get your backpack. Susan said you can come over to help Mommy at work after school. Ruth misses you."

When Robin heard her footsteps on the stairs, her anger returned. "Mother, Dad is gone. We are the only family you have left. Why can't you try to love and accept her? She loves you."

"I've tried watching her after school. I can't," she replied. "You broke our hearts when you decided to have her."

"That's not true. Dad loved her, even if you didn't," she said.

Betty looked at her in disbelief.

"Dad loved you, but you were too angry with God to think about his feelings in my situation. He did not agree with you, but he couldn't hurt you by telling you how he felt. Dad could never share parts of his life with you when he was alive. Now might be a good time for you to find out Dad's true feelings," she said. Without explaining further, she turned and went upstairs.

Robin and Tina returned in a few minutes, and Robin carried a large box.

"This box is from Dad. He wanted me to give it to you on Christmas

Eve, and then he wanted us to go to church together. But I don't think it can wait until Christmas Eve." She placed the box on the kitchen table.

Betty stood staring at the box as they walked out the door.

Robin was very upset, but she wasn't going to let her sweet little girl be affected. She'd never regretted having Tina, and Dad's help after losing Jeff made the difference. Besides, God was always with her. Dad had been with them as much as he could, called daily using a cell phone, and supported her financially if she needed it. They had Skyped often. His business trips were never complete without a visit. He treasured every moment with his grandchild.

"Tina, let's stop and get a quick bite at the cafe before school," Robin said, remembering they had left without breakfast. Tina never complained or demanded anything, but Robin could tell she often sensed the tension at the house. Robin wouldn't let her go to school upset. Tina loved the cafe they frequented most weekends.

The cafe stop had given them alone time and a chance to do their daily prayers. Robin wanted her to do something fun after the confrontation at the house. The Christian school was a great fit, but Tina was still adjusting to the move. After they ate, she dropped Tina off at school and headed to work a couple of miles away. When her mind started to wander back to the kitchen scene, she stopped and prayed, *What is going to happen Lord? My little girl is your gift, and she loves you. She deserves Mom's love too. Lord, I need a miracle ...* The sound of brakes interrupted her thoughts, and then there was darkness.

CHAPTER 9

Betty stared at the box for a long time and wondered about the contents. Could Robin be right, or had she just said that to hurt her? Betty realized it was her own heartless words that were to blame for the confrontation.

Opening the box, she saw what looked like ten numbered scrapbooks. An envelope addressed in a familiar handwriting laid on top of them. With trembling hands she took the letter out.

> To Betty, the love of my life,
>
> I asked Robin to give you this box for Christmas because I knew my cancer would take me by then. This is my last gift, but it is filled with great love. My hope is you will cherish what's in the books. I always had you with me in my heart even when you weren't with me.
>
> You are probably confused and will be upset for a short time, but believe me, what you are about to receive truly is a blessing.
>
> My love for you never wavered during our time together despite the fact you are a very stubborn person. I never understood or agreed with you on how you handled Robin's situation or your rejection of our granddaughter. I tried to reason with you so many times, but you

wouldn't budge. You gave up on God too. I never did. Because those were your two choices alone, I could not share what I was doing. With so many years of blessings from God, perhaps my one regret is not being able to help you trust him to rectify the situation. There is a reason for everything the Lord gives us, and when you look in this box, you will see Robin and Tina were a blessing to me.

Our daughter is a wonderful person and mother. She made the right decision when she chose to keep Tina. Although ten years are gone, you now have your chance to make a difference in their lives. You will find God gave us a gift in Tina. It is time to stop being so concerned about what others think and enjoy the love you've been given.

Enclosed are scrapbooks created by Robin, Tina, and me in hopes of one day sharing them with you to show you how much you missed. You still have a chance to make things right with your family and God.

Christmas is the perfect time for forgiveness and love. God loves you, and he is for you. His love is unconditional. Open your heart to give and receive love.

I always loved you, and I will be looking down on you,

Nate

Betty picked up a scrapbook and noticed they were engraved with a number, Tina's name, and an angel. There were ten of them—one for each year of her life. Each scrapbook contained journaling and pictures of Tina's life. As she flipped through some pages, it was clear Nate hadn't missed any part of it. He'd even attended birthday parties. Pictures included what looked to be a vacation area that the three of them visited together. How was it she never knew? She had been living an empty life with her material possessions, book club, shopping, and bridge. Robin's absence had caused a void, and Nate's job often left her lonely.

The journals were numbered, and she noticed in journal seven, there was a different handwriting and actual drawings. Obviously, Tina and Nate had spent time doing the last three together. She sensed the love through the pages, often marked with little hearts in the corners. A wave of grief and regret came over her because of the loss of being excluded.

There was one hand-drawn picture of the three of them. The label read, "Momma, Poppy, and Me." The detail was amazing. Tina had more ability than she realized. Every day after school, Tina placed a drawing on the counter, and each time Betty stuffed it in a drawer without looking at it. Tears started flowing down her cheeks.

Betty remembered she had seen a picture like this in Nate's wallet once and forgot to ask about it. She went upstairs to look in the wallet, still on his nightstand. The wallet contained several small pictures not labeled with names. Both were labeled with, "I Love U Poppy" in childlike handwriting. Searching the hidden pockets, she found more photos. He had carried them with him every day without her knowing about them.

Betty sat on the bed, and she just cried. All those secrets, but he had been happy. She now realized why. How different things might have been. She hadn't talked to God in all that time either. Would God even want her back? Would he forgive her? Maybe now was the time to take the step back to faith—or was it too late?

"Oh, Robin ... Tina, what have I done?" she cried out.

The phone rang, and Betty sprang to her feet to go around the bed to answer it. She hoped it was Robin. There was so much to say, starting by asking for her forgiveness. Instead, the voice said, "This is Lima General Hospital. I believe Robin Anderson is your daughter?"

"Yes—that's right. What's wrong?" she asked with alarm in her voice.

"I'm afraid your daughter has been in a serious accident, and she's in the emergency room. We will notify Pastor Chris. Can you come quickly?" she asked.

"I'm on my way," she said. "Wait—what about my granddaughter?" she asked.

"Sorry, I only have information on one person. I'll check right now. I'll be at the desk when you arrive. Come quickly!" she said and hung up.

Betty dropped to her knees for the first time in ten years and prayed: *O Lord, not this. This is too much. Please, Lord, I know I don't deserve this but please—give me a chance to make it right. Forgive me!*

She picked up her husband's Bible from his nightstand and headed downstairs. Luckily, the hospital was only minutes away.

When Marilyn interrupted Chris practicing his sermon in the sanctuary with the news that Robin was in serious condition at the hospital and might not make it, he stood in disbelief. In the few times he had encountered Robin and Tina, they had made an impact on him and many other people. Fear gripped him.

Chris hurried to his office and called the school to explain the situation. After calling Kristen to ask if she could pick Tina up, he grabbed his phone and Bible. What would happen if... no, God had his plan. Time would show his purpose for this.

Lima General wasn't far from the church, but he used his Bluetooth to call Marilyn.

"Marilyn, please call the prayer warriors, Susan at the home, and put the prayer request on the website if you can," he said.

She immediately responded, "Already done!"

"Thanks," he said, relieved.

"Keep us posted, and don't you worry, nothing is impossible with our God," she reminded him.

As he hung up, he thanked God for Marilyn.

Inside the emergency room, Chris took a deep breath as he went up to the desk. Someone called his name before he could ask a question.

"Pastor Chris, I'm Betty—Robin's mother. We met at Nate's funeral. Thank you for coming so quickly. Someone's brakes failed, and they slammed into Robin's car. She has a head trauma and is in a coma. The scheduled CT scan will show either a brain injury or a severe concussion. I didn't get a chance to talk to her. I am so sorry. This is my fault," she said, sobbing.

He could see how upset she was, and he asked the nurse for a quiet area. There was an empty consultation room down the hall. The nurse said she would keep them informed of any updates, but it was not possible to see Robin now. Chris opened the door for Betty.

Betty sat down on a chair with tears flowing as she explained the quarrel at home and then Nate's box this morning. It was apparent she wanted and needed reconciliation with her daughter—but would she have a chance? It certainly would end the tension and bitterness between them. Once they were reconciled, they could begin a new relationship, which would include Tina. Chris wondered if Betty truly recognized she had caused her own suffering and unhappiness.

"Tina! Oh, I forgot about Tina!" she said, getting up.

"Thankfully, Tina was already at school. The accident had happened after Robin dropped her off. My wife will be picking her up today after school when she picks up our children. The kids met each other a few times."

"Thank you. I don't know what to tell her."

"It's too early to tell her anything. I can tell you, this is a great hospital, and the staff will get your daughter the best care," he said.

"Actually, Nate went to Rochester for treatment, but I've heard good things from my friends."

They sat for almost an hour without saying a word. Betty was wringing her hands and jumped every time a door opened.

The silence was broken when Chris said, "Betty, now might be the time to talk to God. There's a chapel down the hall."

"I was going to pray for a second chance just before I got the call. I've done so much wrong. Why would he listen? When we found out Robin was pregnant, I prayed for a blessing on Robin and the baby. Instead, he answered by giving her a special needs child. I'm afraid of how he would answer me now," she said.

"Betty, those prayers you prayed years ago were answered. Regrettably, you just didn't accept the gift you had in Tina. Your husband recognized and embraced it. Now is your time to find out how loving she is, but you need to ask God to open your heart to receive it. He will show you how to love like he loves—unconditionally. Ask him."

Betty got up from her chair and headed to the chapel without saying a word. Chris felt certain things would work out in this situation if Betty let God into her life. He prayed it wasn't too late for her to reconcile with her daughter.

CHAPTER 10

Chris waited for over an hour in the emergency room lobby. He used the time to pray for Betty, Robin, and Tina. All thoughts about the sermon, the Christmas Eve service, and the budget seemed insignificant compared to what was going on here.

Betty came down the hall toward Chris. "Any word yet?"

"No, but I'm sure we'll hear soon," he said. "How are you doing?"

"I never realized how much pain and bitterness I kept inside for so long. I cried out to God, and I think the weight of carrying it has lifted. Nate knew how to love more than I did. Bitterness took over, and I deprived myself of experiences I can't get back. My prayer is for an opportunity to express my remorse to Robin."

"Many people are praying for your family right at this moment, and intercessory prayer is powerful," he said. "Christmas is a time for miracles."

A nurse came out to the waiting area and motioned to them. "You can see your daughter now. We've moved her to the ICU. She is not awake. Please understand—she is pretty banged up. Dr. Edwards is waiting to talk to you there. He is a neurosurgeon from the brain trauma unit in Rochester and works here one day a week," she said.

Betty's hands covered her face.

"The fact Dr. Edwards happened to be here today might be an answer to your prayer, Betty," Chris said, trying to free her mind from the gravity of the situation.

Betty looked up at him. Her eyes revealed a willingness to believe and to hope.

Chris gently laid his hand on her back as he led her to the ICU, where Dr. Edwards was waiting.

His face showed his concern. "Your daughter's head trauma is serious, and at this point, we are not sure about a brain injury or how extensive the damage is. We've done a scan, and I am waiting for the results. She is unconscious, and we are not certain when or if she will wake up, but she is in stable condition. I am sorry I can't give you more information at this time," he stated.

"Is she going to die?" Betty asked.

"I'm not sure. It's possible. The sooner she wakes up, the better for her recovery. The next twenty-four hours are critical. She has many minor cuts and abrasions, but we ruled out internal injuries, which is good. Go in and talk to her even though she is not awake. In our experience, unconscious patients recognize familiar voices."

"Thank you," Betty said.

She paused before entering the room and took a deep breath. She sat in the chair next to the bed. Robin's head was bandaged, her eyes were swollen, and bruises covered her arms and face. Chris stood in the doorway in case he was needed. Her breathing was labored as she sought to compose herself. Finally, she reached out and gently took Robin's hand and began pouring her heart out, hoping her words would reach her little girl.

Chris left her alone, knowing Betty had so much to tell her daughter. He stopped at the nurse's station to make sure Betty had support before he left.

When Chris reached the door to the parking garage, he turned his cell phone back on. Kristen had texted him: *What about Tina? What do I tell her?*

He texted back: *On my way. I will talk to her.*

It was already dark out. Tina would know something was up, and he would have to explain why Robin or Betty weren't coming. This was probably the hardest thing he had to do.

When Chris entered the kitchen, Kristen and the children were all making Christmas cookies. Tina looked like she was enjoying herself. The colored sprinkles and frosting were all spread around the table. They all sang along with the Christmas CD playing as they frosted. They were so happy, so innocent, and he didn't want to interrupt.

Chris and Kristen moved away from the table.

"How is Robin?" Kristen whispered.

"She is unconscious. The doctors aren't sure how serious her injuries are," he answered. "Does Tina act like she thinks something is wrong?"

"It's hard to say how aware she is of time. She's such a sweet little thing. I was grateful we had a chance to meet her a few weeks ago."

"She looks pretty comfortable around Robbie and Chloe."

"We've had a good time. I noticed she is so creative, even in the decorating. I researched Down syndrome, and it is rare for children to be able to sing or draw like she can but not impossible." she said.

"God gives us all different talents. Do you mind if she stays here for a few days?" he asked.

"Of course not. She can stay as long as she needs to. The kids love playing with her, and she takes care of herself. But you will need to tell her something soon," she responded.

"That's why I came home. Betty needed alone time with Robin," he said.

"By the way, were you aware someone made a video of Tina singing at the home Sunday and posted it on YouTube? Ten thousand hits so far," she said.

"Really? There was someone using their phone to record, but I never would have guessed they would post it on YouTube," Chris said.

When they finished decorating, Chris said, "Tina, Pastor Chris needs to talk to you for a minute. Would you come in here to talk with me please?"

Tina bit her lower lip and looked to Kristen first before getting up. Her usual smile was gone, and she continued biting her lip, following him into the family room. She looked back to Kristen several times but kept going.

"Honey, Momma won't be home tonight. She's sick, so you are going to need to stay here," he said.

"Sick? I can help Momma. I'm a good helper," she said.

"I know you are, but this time Momma hurt her head, and only the doctors at a hospital know what to do. Momma needs to stay there for a while," he said.

"Will she be going with Poppy?" she asked.

Chris realized that she understood what death was. He could only answer, "We all need to pray for Momma."

Tina grabbed the heart necklace she had around her neck. "Poppy and Momma are always here, and Jesus." She opened the necklace, and on one side was a picture of the three of them. The other side had a picture of Jesus.

Holding the locket, she began to sing, "Jesus Loves Me."

Singing was her way of praying too.

His cell phone rang, and he saw from caller ID it was Betty.

"Hello, Betty—any change?" he asked.

"No change yet. I'm sorry I forgot about Tina again—today was surreal. I am so confused and …"

"Betty—she's fine here tonight, and she can stay here until you are up to taking her home. Your daughter needs you. Let us care for Tina. Call if things change, and remember, many people are praying for Robin," he said.

He could hear her crying softly and asked, "Betty, did you get something to eat?"

"Molly's here with me now, and she brought dinner. She said church members will be taking turns to stay with me tonight. I want to stay nearby."

"I'm glad you are not alone. Do you mind if I speak with Molly?" he asked.

"Sure."

"Chris, I am staying for a while, and between the workers at the home and church members, Betty will not be alone tonight. Our deacons are at church now holding a prayer vigil too."

"Thanks, we are going to pray after we settle the children in. I don't want to alarm Tina, although her body language tells me she is worried. Poor little thing," he said. "Call me with any word, please."

"I will, and Chris, people have called Marilyn all day asking for ways to help. That YouTube video was on the news with the accident report. Some of the families out of work are calling to help too. Amazing."

"Indeed. Talk to you soon," he said, hanging up the phone.

In all his years of being a pastor, he certainly had faced many tragedies and deaths, but the fact the congregation stepped right in gave him a sense of divine intervention.

Lord, thanks for your help! Be with Betty and Robin. Please give them a chance to be the family they were meant to be.

CHAPTER 11

Chris and Kristen agreed to keep things as normal as possible for Tina. Kristen had been a substitute teacher in her class and was familiar with the daily schedule. Tina believed Jesus would take care of Robin, and they didn't want to alarm her.

Before going to the hospital the next day, Chris stopped at the church to check on pressing matters and possibly work on his upcoming sermons. Molly greeted him at the door.

"Chris—I stayed with Betty for a few hours last night, and she even let me pray with her. Other members are taking turns today, and she won't be alone. Betty used to be quite active in church activities, and Marilyn helped me reach out to people she knew. Debbie volunteered to stay the night and will be there until you arrive."

"I can't thank you enough, Molly. She needs encouragement and support. Any word on Robin?"

"Debbie called to say she is in stable condition but is still unconscious."

"The doctor said the first twenty-four hours were critical."

"Chris, my timing is bad."

"What's on your mind?" he asked.

"I still don't have children to sing on Christmas Eve. What are we going to do?" she asked.

"Keep praying," he said. "If it comes down to it, we can all sing Christmas carols together. Robin's situation is grave, and the soloist situation seems less important. Molly, I want you believe things will work out."

Molly didn't respond, and her face didn't convey confidence.

Chris tried to encourage her by saying, "Kristen is going to bring the kids over to help you start with Christmas Eve preparations after school. Tina is staying with us, so she is coming too. She loves to draw—put her to good use," he said with a smile. "Believe."

"We sure can use the help this year," she replied. "Several of my volunteers are at the hospital to support Betty today. The ICU will only let family in, but I have someone in the waiting area praying constantly."

"Thanks. Maybe I can work on my sermon before I go over. Molly, remember—simple," he added.

Even though his office was quiet, Chris wasn't able to concentrate on his sermon. Although he was optimistic for Molly's sake, the other members of the congregation needed cheering up this season. He closed his eyes.

Lord, help me to find the words to reach the less fortunate this Advent. Your people are hurting, and many have lost their spirit. I ask that your Spirit fill me with words in these coming weeks to open their hearts to recognize your gift is the greatest one they will receive. I ask this in the name of Jesus. Amen.

For quite a few minutes, he sat and listened, waiting until he sensed a soft whisper. *All is well. My grace will be sufficient. Think of the less fortunate.*

Less fortunate—Chris now felt he had a direction for his sermon, and it fit the season. An hour later he had a draft of the sermon ready and notes for the next few weeks.

Chris decided to head over to the hospital after he finished his sermons. He found Betty by Robin's bedside and observed the journals on table.

"Are these the journals your husband made of your granddaughter's life?" he asked.

"Yes, they are. I've been reading them to Robin in hopes they would stimulate her memory and wake her up. The details are so vivid and certainly not how I envisioned Robin's life would be. How foolish I feel," she said, shaking her head. She looked worn out, but there was love in her eyes when she looked at her daughter.

Chris did not know what to say. Betty had tried to control what only God could control. The journal entries and pictures showed a beautiful love story of a mother, grandfather, and granddaughter.

"Not only did I miss time with them, but I lost time with Nate too. How could I not know what he was doing?"

"Has the neurosurgeon been in yet?" he asked, trying to change the subject.

"Yes. No change yet. We just need to wait. Making it through the night was good news," she said

"Betty, one day at a time. I wanted you to know Kristen will pick Tina up from school and bring her to the church to help with Christmas Eve preparations. Shall we keep her overnight again?" he asked.

"Yes—thank you! I want to keep going through these books with my Robin. I need to be here if she wakes," she said.

"Remember to take a break. We can't have you getting run down. Someone is always in the waiting area," he said. "Call me later."

Chris thought about how sometimes God uses a crisis to get our attention and remind us that he is the one in control. The Bible is full of people who let their pride ruin God's plan for them. But God is a Redeemer.

On the drive back to the church, he passed the Christmas tree lot, and the streets were bustling with shoppers. The season was in full swing, and Christmas would be here soon. He prayed that this change in Betty would help her rediscover the true meaning of Christmas.

CHAPTER 12

The fellowship hall became a hub of activity after school. Molly and some elders were painting backgrounds for the Christmas Eve service. Following Chris's advice, worship wouldn't be complicated, and the focus would be on the shepherds and the birth of Jesus. The volunteers were comprised of a mix of church members. Between the hospital and the church, members just showed up, which helped fill Molly with hope. The service would be simple, with the few children they had and maybe a couple of adults.

Kristen was painting scenery with Chloe and Robbie when Chris came in. Tina was off to the side coloring by herself. Chris waved to his wife and went over to talk to Tina. Her picture was a very detailed picture of a group of angels. When one angel was clearly labeled "Poppy," he realized Tina was thinking about heaven. She rocked in place and didn't notice his presence. Remembering how she loved music, he found Molly and asked her to put some Christmas music on.

Tina's mood changed with the music, and she sang while coloring. Everyone in the hall stopped working and listened.

"Chris, what do you think about Tina singing on Christmas Eve?" Molly asked.

At first he didn't respond. It had never occurred to him that Tina would sing. "I'm not sure; Robin will need to decide for her. She still isn't awake. I thought about taking her over to visit Robin, but I don't think she would understand what a coma is. Poor little thing—she's had so much change lately. If things aren't better soon, we'll need to prepare her," he said.

Tina continued to sing "Away in a Manger" as she colored. When she got up to get a drink, the finished drawing laid on the table. Molly took the opportunity to look at what she'd done.

When Tina came back, Molly was holding her picture.

"Tina, this is a great picture. Tell me about it."

Tina took the picture and described every detail. It was clear she believed in heaven and angels. Musical notes surrounded them.

"Would you mind if we used your picture for Christmas Eve service? It is so special, and I think everyone would want to see it on the big screen. What do you think?"

For the first time that day, Tina's lips curved into a small smile. She nodded yes and handed her picture back to Molly.

Chloe and Robbie ran over to them.

Robbie said, "Tina, we're getting our Christmas tree tonight. Do you want to help us pick out a tree and decorate tonight?"

"Sure," she answered. Her face lit up.

"We can pick a big one this year! Let's get our coats," Chloe said, taking her hand.

They all ran hand in hand to the coat rack.

Kristen came over to Molly. "Keeping her busy is working for now. Looks like some good progress today."

Molly looked around the hall. "Today has given me hope for our program. Things are taking shape without my usual detailed plan."

Her remark made Kristen laugh. "Molly, surrender. It's *his* plan this year. We always forget that! We're off to the tree lot. We'll be back tomorrow."

A few miles away at the hospital, Betty was still going through the scrapbooks with Robin, hoping to see a sign of her waking up. Reading each one slowly was also for her own benefit. Tina had been involved in the same activities Robin had done as a child. There were pictures of her dancing, singing, swinging, riding a bike, and playing sports. Nate was in many of them. Several pictures included church activities. Tina had been part of several church Christmas pageants beginning at age three. Betty stepped out to the waiting room as the nurse came in to do vitals and change IVs.

Ellen, one of her bridge partners and a church member, sat praying. "I'm glad you're taking a break. You look exhausted."

Betty responded, "I am. Waiting is hard." She wiped her eyes. "As difficult as this situation is, the outpouring of support and compassion is appreciated. I could not do this by myself."

"Good. We will be here for whatever you need. I brought dinner too. Let's say grace and then make sure you eat to keep up your strength. Betty, you will also need to go home to rest. One night here is enough. I will stay and let you know if anything changes."

Betty knew she was right. She forced herself to eat despite the churning in her stomach. When she ate all she could, she said, "Ellen, I am going in to say good night to Robin."

The ICU was quiet, with only the sound of machines. She looked at Robin and said, "I love you, honey. You have to wake up. We need you." She squeezed her hand and looked for some sign that she felt it, but nothing happened.

The nurse on duty felt helpless watching her, knowing the pain situations like this caused families. Each case was different, and she had witnessed both tragedy and total recovery. She entered the room and said, "Tomorrow's another day. Is it all right to give information to your friend?"

"Yes. She'll call me."

"See you in the morning."

Betty walked out to the parking garage disheartened.

CHAPTER 13

When Betty arrived at the ICU the next morning, the nurse came up to her. "Your daughter has a visitor, but our policy is only family, clergy, and authorized visitors. I asked the young lady to wait over there."

Betty looked over in the small waiting room and recognized Marcy.

"Hello, Marcy. I'm sorry I didn't call. So much happened," she said.

"I heard about the accident when I tried to call Robin at work this week. She was supposed to call me about Christmas shopping, but when she didn't return my call, I got worried."

"This is the third day of her coma. I don't know if she will wake up. I have so much to tell her, I'm …" She choked up.

"Mrs. Johnson, I'm here to help. I took some time off, and I am here for you too. Where's Tina?"

"She's been staying with the pastor's family. During the day, she is at school. I'm afraid we haven't bonded. How long have you known Robin?"

"We've been friends since before she had Tina. She loves being a mom. Did you notice Tina called me Aunt Marcy at Thanksgiving?"

"No, I didn't. Marcy, I want to apologize for not being friendly on Thanksgiving. I can't fix the past, but I want to change the future. Maybe you can help me with Tina. You are welcome to stay at the house, if you would like to."

"I might take you up on that. First, I would like to visit Robin. Would that be all right?"

"Sure." Betty led her to the ICU.

Marcy's facial expressions showed she was startled by what she saw, but she didn't say anything.

Betty met with the doctor, and although there was no change, the scans didn't indicate brain swelling. Robin's color was coming back to her cheeks.

Betty relayed the update to Marcy.

"Betty, I can sit with Robin if you have errands to do. Do you have food for Tina? You've been by her side for days."

"I wanted to be here if she woke up."

"I can call your cell if she does."

Betty thought for a few minutes and then said, "You're right. Tina needs to come home. I'll pick up some things, and I'll be back in a few hours. Thank you." She wrote her cell number on the pad next to the bed. "Call me."

"I will," Marcy said.

Betty knew she had to bring Tina home.

The afternoon was more of the same for everyone. Kristen took the children over to church to work on more painting.

Chris walked in to speak to Kristen. "Betty called from ICU. Robin isn't waking up, but she is going to come to get Tina after dinner."

"Are you sure she's ready for that?" Kristen asked.

"Robin's close friend Marcy is here, and she's going to help. I think that's a good thing," he said.

"Good. I think Betty could use support from someone who knows Tina."

"Let's wait to tell Tina until they pick her up. I think she will be happy to see Marcy."

Betty returned from grocery shopping and spent the afternoon in the ICU with Marcy at her side. The time passed quickly, and Marcy was able to fill Betty in with some of the details of the pictures in the scrapbooks.

When Robin hadn't shown any signs of waking up, Betty began to worry. She picked up the last of the journals and found a manila envelope labeled:

To Momma

From: Poppy and Tina

The envelope contained what appeared to be a music CD.

A nurse came in to check Robin's vitals and saw the CD.

"You know, when people are unconscious, familiar music does stimulate the brain. Sometimes they respond and start moving. We don't have a CD player, but you can bring one in," she said.

Betty looked at the clock and saw the late hour. There wasn't time to come back.

"I'll bring one over tomorrow. I'll also be bringing my granddaughter after we go to church," she said as she put her coat on. Then she turned to Marcy. "Shall we go pick up Tina?"

"Can we drop my car at your house first?" she asked.

"That makes sense," Betty said. "Good night. Call us if anything changes."

"I will," said the nurse.

Marcy followed Betty to her home. When Marcy didn't pull into the driveway, Betty pulled in and walked over.

"You can park your car in the driveway. There's enough room."

"Betty, I just thought this might be an emotional time for you and Tina. I think it's best if I drive you over. What do you think?" she asked.

Marcy was right. Betty seemed nervous, and the ride was quiet except for the directions.

"Betty, I'm here for you. You'll be fine. Robin had fond memories of her childhood. You'll be a good grandmother."

"I hope so. I've made many mistakes."

"Open your heart to love, Betty. Tina only needs love."

They rang the bell, and Chris answered.

"Welcome. Come on in. The kids and Kristen are finishing up the tree."

When Tina looked up, her eyes lit up. To Betty's surprise, she ran over and hugged her first. Then she went over to Marcy. She chatted with Marcy about the tree for a few minutes, and then Tina asked, "Where's Momma?"

"Momma's still sick, honey, and needs to rest, but tomorrow you'll visit after church. Would you like to go home with Marcy and me?" Betty asked.

"Uh-huh," she said.

After her goodbyes, Tina took Betty's hand and went to gather her things.

Chris whispered to Marcy, "What a precious child. We've enjoyed having her. It is so good of you to come support Betty."

"She does need it. So tragic to be waiting and wondering if someone will wake up from a coma," she added.

"It's been a long week, that's for sure," he said. "Good night. See you in church?"

"I hope so. Good night and thanks. I don't know a pastor who would have taken on an extra child," she added.

"She's an angel and been no trouble at all. I'm sure you already knew that."

CHAPTER 14

Chris arrived at church an hour before the service. He had prepared his sermon yesterday, but this morning he sensed God leading him in another direction. The few days his family spent with Tina reminded him of how God's love can shine through the children. He decided that more time praying for Robin was needed. His early morning e-mail described the change in the service to members.

Entering the sanctuary, he was startled to see how many people were there. He recognized several people who worked at the group home, but the pews were filled with many people he'd never seen before. His wife and children sat in the front row. Betty, Tina, and Marcy joined them as the organ was about to play the prelude. He couldn't help but smile.

The sermon spoke about Christmas miracles and the childlike faith needed when a situation seemed hopeless. The message included an emphasis on love. Advent's message of hope in the child born in the manger clearly was related to Robin's situation. After his sermon, Chris introduced Tina and Betty. He asked everyone to bow their heads as they prayed for Robin's complete recovery.

He concluded by asking Tina, "Would you would like to say anything?"

Tina thought for a moment and asked, "Can we sing Momma's favorite song?"

"What would that song be?" he questioned.

"Shine, Jesus, Shine," she answered.

Chris looked at Molly, and she went to the piano.

As she started to play, Tina began to sing. Her soft little voice filled the sanctuary, and she never noticed that no one sang with her. She was singing to Jesus and thinking about her mom. There wasn't a dry eye in the house.

The service ended with the usual benediction. The song overwhelmed Betty.

Marcy motioned to her. "Betty, let's go out this way," she said, pointing to the old side entrance for choir members.

Chris stood at the exit shaking hands with people on their way to the fellowship hall.

Molly came over as the last person passed and said, "Tina is going to the hospital with Betty to visit her mom."

"I know, and I think that's good," he said. Then he asked, "Molly, what brought so many people to church today? Surely it's not my sermons bringing them here."

"Actually, the YouTube video. The video has gone viral, with over twenty-five thousand hits. People have called the office and the home all week asking if Tina went to church here."

"Amazing," he said, shaking his head.

Kristen walked up and asked, "Coming home soon?"

"Very soon, but I want to make a stop at the hospital first," he answered.

Betty buckled Tina into her seat belt. She couldn't believe she was driving her granddaughter someplace. Marcy sat in the passenger seat, letting Betty handle Tina by herself.

When they reached the hospital garage, she asked Tina to wait as she got the CD player from the trunk and could help her unbuckle. She wasn't taking any chances with this precious child.

Betty took Tina's hand and said, "Let's go see Momma."

On the walk to the ICU, Betty said softly to Tina, "Now when we see

Momma, she will still be sleeping, so she won't be able to talk. I need you to be a big girl. Can you do that?"

Tina nodded her head but looked worried.

The nurse let them all in. They noticed Robin's color had come back to her face. Betty plugged the player in and put the CD from the box in to play.

Tina's eyes lit up when she recognized Poppy and her singing on the CD. She hadn't heard these songs since last Christmas. Momma had loved their gift.

As the music played, she took her mother's hand and waited. The nurses in the ICU all watched and listened to the music too. Tina stroked her hand and hummed too. Robin's eyelids began to flutter, and she squeezed Tina's hand.

"Momma, wake up, please," Tina pleaded.

Robin slowly opened her eyes and looked around at her surroundings. Her eyes finally focused on Betty, who was smiling at her.

"Robin, you're in the hospital. You were in a car accident. Someone ran a stop sign when their brakes failed. You have a head injury and need to stay still," Betty explained.

"Mom—Tina?"

"Don't worry. Look who is holding your hand," she said.

It took time for Robin to get oriented. She smiled at Tina and looked back at her mom. "Mom, I am so sorry."

"For …?" Betty realized she remembered the fight. But how? "No, I'm the one who is sorry, but we don't need to talk now. There will be lots of time for catching up when you are better. This little angel has waited a long time for you to wake up. And look who else is here."

Robin looked over and saw Marcy. "Two visits in one month?"

They all laughed.

Tina and Robin chatted for a few minutes. Robin looked over to the nearby chair. "Mom—are those the journals? Did you look at them?"

"Yes, I went through each one. So many memorable moments I missed, but I'm not missing any more time," she said.

"I'm glad," Robin said. "Mom, we need you."

"Good, because I need you both. Now that you're awake, it looks like the doctor is here to talk about your injuries," Betty said as she motioned for him to come in

Dr. Edwards came in the room. "I'm Dr. Edwards. You're a lucky person. My newest scan shows no brain injury or concussion. I'm not sure what caused the coma. You do have bruising, so you'll be sore. You should rest."

"When can she go home?" Betty asked.

"Robin would be able to go home by tomorrow, but she needs to take a few weeks off from work and strenuous activities. It's best to be cautious."

Betty turned to Robin and said, "Marcy, Tina and I need to go home and decorate so we are ready for tomorrow. We'll be here early to take you home. I'm going to let Tina miss one day of school. The doctor wants you to rest now. I love you!"

Robin blinked back tears.

"Momma, love you!" Tina said as she blew a kiss.

Betty, Tina, and Marcy were deep in conversation planning what they needed to do as they left the ICU. They didn't notice Chris in the waiting room or the other man sitting there. Chris jumped up and stopped them to ask about Robin. Because Robin was resting, he decided to wait on his visit and go to the chapel to give thanks to God instead. Oddly, the young man was gone when he passed the waiting room.

CHAPTER 15

Marcy, Betty, and Tina stopped at the Christmas tree lot on the way home.

"Tina, we need a tree—a *big* tree. Can you help me find one?" Betty asked.

The lot was full of beautiful trees. Betty thought she would skip the tree this year, but Robin's accident had changed everything.

"Looks like this little one is serious about getting the perfect tree," said the tree attendant. "I'm John, Molly's husband."

Betty recognized him from the church service.

"I usually let Nate pick the tree. I'm new at this," she responded.

"Nate was the same way as Tina is about the tree. Let me see if I can help her. As I recall, he always picked a Frazier fir?" he asked.

"Yes, he did."

"Here, Grandma—here," Tina yelled from down the walkway.

Marcy and Tina stood next to a large Frazier fir. Their faces awaited Betty's approval.

"Wow, looks like the perfect tree. What do you think, Marcy?" she asked.

"I think it is the best one in this lot. Do you have enough decorations?" Marcy asked.

"John, can you hold this tree? I think we need to pick up a few things," Betty asked.

"I can do better than that. If you don't mind a little wait, my helper is coming at five o'clock. I can stop by with the tree after that," he said.

Betty looked at her watch. It was two o'clock, and they needed to eat plus pick up a few decorations.

"Great! That helps so much," Betty said. "Do you know where I live?"

"Sure, Nate was a regular, and I've delivered your trees before."

Betty paid John and turned to Marcy and Tina. "Our tree will need more decorations."

"Momma has decorations," Tina said.

"Why don't we stop at the cafe for a quick bite, and then we'll look for the decorations at home?" Betty thought back to the Christmas trees in the scrapbooks. Each one was beautiful, and Nate was in each picture.

"Betty, it's time to make new memories," Marcy said.

"I know, but that doesn't mean it will be easy."

"He'll be in your heart. Remember, all of you are grieving. Nate would want life to go on. Let's get that lunch. I'm starving!"

The fully decorated cafe reminded them of the season, and they enjoyed the lunch. Marcy was surprised by the change in Betty. She treated Tina affectionately, and an outsider would not question her genuine love for her granddaughter. Several patrons recognized Tina and commented on her singing. Betty beamed with pride.

John arrived promptly at five and offered to put the tree in the stand and also put the lights on. The tree was huge, but the family room had enough space for it.

Molly arrived with a large pizza, ready to help where she was needed.

"Robin's boxes are in the basement, and my decorations are in the attic," Betty said.

"Let's go down and find your decorations," Marcy said to Tina.

"Betty, John and I will go up to the attic with you."

They worked together, and the boxes filled the room. Tina helped find Robin's decorations and waited in anticipation as John put the lights on before going back to the tree lot. When the lights were turned on, Tina's eyes opened wide with amazement, and she stood in awe. Betty cherished the moment as her thoughts went back to Robin's childhood. Robin loved to turn all the family room lights off and watch the twinkling lights on the tree.

After several minutes, Betty said, "What beautiful lights! Don't you think so, Tina?"

She giggled and said, "They're so pretty! Momma's going to love them."

Molly began to help Betty carefully unpack her treasures. Her eyes watered many times as she placed ornaments on the tree. She tried to conceal her grief. Tina stopped decorating and took Betty's hand.

"Poppy's here," she said, pointing to her heart. Betty hugged her and let the tears flow—tears of both happiness and grief.

"Maybe we should finish tomorrow when Robin comes home? Then she can be a part of it," Marcy said. "We can make her comfy on the couch."

"Good idea. Now, who wants pizza?" Molly asked.

"Me," said Tina.

"Me," said Marcy.

"I'll be along in a minute," Betty said. She sat in her chair with an ornament Nate had purchased last Christmas.

Nate, I am so sorry. I hope you're looking down tonight. I do feel you here in my heart. I have my daughter and granddaughter back. You have your wish.

CHAPTER 16

Robin came home the next day. The bruising left her with pain in her arms and legs. Before Dr. Edwards discharged her, he reminded her that she needed two weeks of rest and cautioned her about strenuous activity. If she followed orders, she would be able to attend Christmas Eve service.

"Doctor, she will be well taken care of, and she will follow your orders," Betty said assertively. "Right, Tina?"

"I'm helping Grandma," Tina said.

"Seems like I have no choice but to rest." Robin laughed.

Marcy stayed for one more day but had to go back to work. The rest of the decorating was finished. They combined both Betty's and Robin's holiday decor. For the first time in months, Robin felt like it was her home too.

Tina reluctantly went to school on Tuesday, which left Betty and Robin alone.

Robin settled in on the couch, and Betty busied herself in the kitchen, occasionally checking on her. Just before lunch, Robin called her.

"Mom, can you come in here please?"

"Did you need something? I'll make lunch soon."

"I want to talk."

Betty sat in her chair and looked apprehensively at Robin.

"Mom, I really appreciate all you've done. I can't imagine Tina and me going through this without you."

"You don't need to thank me."

"Mom, we need to all grieve together. I wish I could go back in time and do things differently with you."

"What do you mean?"

"My pride stopped me from calling you and trying to mend our relationship."

"Robin, I was the one who was wrong. We can't fix the past. Chris told me that God's plans are not always our plans, but he is faithful with a purpose for our lives."

"That's right. When I'm back on my feet, I want to be more involved at the church. How about you? I remember how involved you used to be."

"The outpouring of generosity from church members during your coma reminded me of the community of faith I lost. I stopped everything because I was mad at God. The same people I turned my back on supported me through those difficult days."

"Are you still mad?" Robin asked.

"No. Your accident made me realize life is precious and good. I asked him for forgiveness and thanked him for not answering my prayer. Looking through your journals, I saw God's faithfulness in your life."

"What prayer do you mean—Tina?" Robin asked

Betty paused and stared at Robin's face.

"I don't want you upset. Hear me out. Yes—Tina. I know it sounds cold, but let me explain my reasons."

"I'm listening." *God give me patience,* Robin prayed silently.

"I never told anyone this, even your father. My cousin Vinnie had Down syndrome. We were the same age."

"What happened?"

"When I entered school, it was embarrassing to be with him around my friends. They called him names and taunted him. I didn't want to lose my friends, so I distanced myself from him."

"Where is he now?"

"Vinnie had a heart defect and died when he was eight. I'm not proud of the way I acted."

"Mom, you were a child."

"Still, I regret the fact I never told him how sorry I was. I loved him, and his death devastated me. When you told me about your baby, I didn't want you to go through the heartache of losing a child or people making fun of your child."

"Why didn't you ever tell me this?"

"Shame."

"Faith in Jesus will help rid you of your shame."

"Now that I'm being honest, I thought Tina was God's way of punishing me for how I treated Vinnie."

"God disciplines, but you were a child. Tina is a blessing to us all, not a punishment. Mom, when you know God's true character, you will learn to trust. My life seemed to spiraling out of control after Jeff left. My Christian community and Dad helped me see God had control and I needed to trust. He was faithful to his promises of a life better than I could imagine."

"You're remarkable. After the holidays, I want to join a Bible study and see where it leads. I admire your faith and would like to be in a community of believers. Now I need to finish making lunch, and I want you to rest. I hope you're hungry."

"I am, and Mom ..."

"Yes?"

"Thanks for your honesty."

Betty smiled as she got up from her chair.

Robin lowered her head. *Lord, thank you for helping Mom unburden herself. Speak to her through your word, and teach her to forgive herself.*

The week before Christmas was busy. As Robin recovered church and community members continued to give support. Kristen stopped by with containers of decorated cookies. Susan stopped by with more pizza and to ask if Tina could sing one more time at the home. Robin agreed, thinking it would be good for Tina and the residents. Marilyn stopped to offer to babysit for Robin and Tina sometime on Monday so Betty could buy Christmas presents. Other members of the church dropped off food for Christmas Eve dinner and Christmas day. Betty was impressed at their free giving during their own busy times. With two days until Christmas, Betty felt like Christmas had already come.

Robin followed the doctor's orders carefully because she didn't want to miss the Christmas Eve service. Tina was singing a solo. As she gained strength, she helped Betty wrap presents.

Susan took Tina to the home, and she delighted the residents with songs again. Ruth's daughter was happy to see her mom play with such joy again.

With Tina gone, Robin found another chance to talk frankly with Betty.

Robin said, "Mom, how are you doing with all this Christmas activity?"

"Christmas is as exhausting as ever, but I am looking forward to Christmas with you and Tina. Dinner will be a combination of what people brought over and what I am making."

"I mean, how are you doing with Dad being gone?"

Her question startled Betty. "There is not a day that goes by that I don't miss him. I'm taking it one day at a time. I do know I couldn't make it without you being here."

"Although Dad never spent Christmas with Tina and me, we did have our own celebration. But you know that."

"He hid it well. The journals are great way of traveling back in time to all I missed. Maybe we should go through your old photo albums over the school recess."

"Where are they? I don't remember them."

"Your father has always kept scrapbooks. He put them in the attic when we had our falling out because he knew they would be reminders of you. He actually thought I would throw them out."

"I'm glad you didn't, and think how great it would be for Tina to see them."

"Robin, there is only one problem."

"What?"

"Jeff is in some of the albums."

Robin's smile quickly vanished.

"Does she know about Jeff?" Betty asked.

"How would I explain her father not wanting her? He doesn't know about her, and I never said anything to her."

Betty could see Robin shaking and on the verge of tears.

"We can decide after Christmas. Let's enjoy each other and not worry needlessly," Betty said. "I'm going to make some tea for us."

Robin watched her go to the kitchen. *Father, what do I tell her about Jeff? Please help me protect her from any more pain.*

CHAPTER 17

Marilyn burst into Chris's office Monday morning without knocking. Before he could say a word, she started. "Chris, you are not going to believe this. The counters reported that they received many sizable donations in the collection plate yesterday. Two of them were for fifty thousand dollars each. I called the banks, and the checks are good. Your sermon and Tina's singing apparently stirred some emotions."

Chris looked at her in disbelief and then began to laugh out loud. "Wait until John hears that! I told him God would provide, and he did. The usher count indicated abnormally high numbers too. Tina displayed a faith to be admired by others. God has answered so many prayers these past two weeks!"

Marilyn couldn't help herself. "Well he is a *big God* and he does *big things*!" She turned to leave but paused as she turned around and said, "I don't think he is done yet. The Christmas Eve service might be better yet!"

Molly picked Tina up at 10:00 a.m. on Christmas Eve to practice. The children were going to act out the Christmas story. Tina would be dressed as an angel and sing "Silent Night." The service would end with candlelight while Tina sang. Molly stood in awe listening to Tina's solo. The other children cheered her on when she finished.

Molly reflected back to her initial worry and looked up to the cross, saying, "*Amen!* Boys and girls, I am so proud of you. Remember to be here at five thirty to prepare."

The service began promptly at 6:00 p.m. The sanctuary was completely full. Betty and Robin sat in the front row with Kristen. Chris gave a short sermon on the most generous and greatest gift we receive at Christmas—Jesus Christ. Cloe and Robbie played Mary and Joseph. Marilyn narrated as the children acted out the nativity story. Tina looked beautiful in the angel outfit surrounded by a few small shepherds and other angels. At the last minute, several families stepped up to participate in the truest spirit of Christmas, choosing to forget their own problems and focus on worship of Jesus.

Molly dimmed the lights and turned on the projector, and Tina's drawing of angels was projected on the screen behind Tina for her solo. Strands of lights twinkled around the manger scene with Mary and Joseph. The sky backdrop on the manger also twinkled with lights. Each person in the sanctuary held a lit candle, and Tina sang, "Silent Night." The simplicity of the program revealed the truest of Christmas messages.

Kristen and Chris watched the sanctuary empty. God had provided, and the community celebrated the birth of Christ forgetting their own problems.

"What a lovely service!" Kristen said. "Betty acted like such a doting grandmother. That family has been through so much."

Chris agreed and added, "Nate would be pleased, and I hope he is watching from heaven. Let me lock the front doors and check the others. I'll be home soon." Kristen kissed him on the cheek and went to the narthex, where Chloe and Robbie waited with Molly.

A young man stepped out of the dark corner. Chris recognized him from the hospital.

"Hi. I didn't want to interrupt," he said.

Chris asked, "Didn't I see you at the hospital?"

"I was in the waiting room of the ICU. That was a powerful service. I haven't been to church in over ten years."

"What brought you here tonight?" Chris asked.

"I watched a video online of a little girl singing. I also saw someone in the video that I think is my ex-wife, Robin Anderson. I'm Jeff Anderson."

"Did Robin invite you?" he asked.

"No—she didn't know I was here."

"What do you want?"

"I'm not sure, but Tina might be my daughter."

"Why come back now?"

"Is Tina my daughter?" he asked.

"You'll have to talk to Robin."

Jeff paused, and his facial expression suggested shock. "I thought if I left and she was alone, she might get the abortion." He kept rubbing the back of his neck and clearly was conflicted. Then he asked, "Do you really think Christmas is a time for miracles?"

Chris looked at the sanctuary cross, and he locked the door. "I certainly do, Jeff. Would you like to talk?"

Jeff nodded, and they walked down the hall to Chris's office.

CHAPTER 18

Opening his office door, Chris invited Jeff in. Jeff seemed nervous but genuinely overcome with emotion. Chris looked at the small nativity scene on his desk, such a miracle. Was God working another one now?

Jeff sat facing Chris with his eyes also on the nativity.

"Do you mind if I ask a personal question?" Chris asked.

"No, I guess not."

"Jeff, are you a Christian?"

"Robin and I were married in a church, and we did go to church on Sundays," he answered.

"But did you have a relationship with Jesus?"

"I don't even know what that means. I went to church for Robin."

It was clear Jeff wasn't really saved, and neither did he understand what he meant. Still, Chris wanted to dig deeper.

"Since you and Robin separated, have you been to church?"

"I haven't set a foot into a church until today. When I found out the prenatal testing showed a possible Down syndrome baby, I made a decision to never go to church again. How would God allow a young couple to face such a dilemma? It just shouldn't happen."

"God allows circumstances for his own purposes. Understanding them can be difficult at the time. How long did you stand in the back of the church?"

"The whole service," he answered.

Obviously, most attendees were moved by the program and Tina's solo. "How did you feel?" Chris asked.

Jeff hesitated and struggled to answer. "Honestly, I kept thinking—is she mine? I never expected such a sweet voice."

"Would you want her to be your daughter?"

"At that moment, yes. I didn't think the video on YouTube could be real."

"Who told you about the video?"

"Everyone in my office was talking about a video that went viral. I watched it and thought I recognized Robin."

"Go on."

"The camera only showed her briefly while panning the audience. She looked so beautiful and happy. We used to be happy until …"

"Until the pregnancy?" Chris asked.

"Yes, everything changed after her test results. Our whole future changed in an instant."

"Meaning?"

"A lifetime of difficulties. This caused such a wedge between us. I had to leave—don't you see?"

"Difficulties? I'm not judging, but how familiar did you become with the option of keeping the baby?"

"For me there wasn't another choice, and Robin was so emotional. Our arguing never led to an answer. I left. I never heard from her after I walked out."

"You knew Robin had the accident though. You were waiting at the hospital to hear her prognosis?"

"I called the home after the video and said I wanted to give the child singing a donation. They eagerly gave me the contact information but informed me Robin was in the ICU."

"What was your reaction?"

"I immediately booked a flight. I was so afraid she would die before we could talk," Jeff said, and then he stopped. "Oh, I'm sorry. It's Christmas Eve, and I'm taking up so much of your time."

"Actually, my family is waiting. You asked if Christmas could be a time for miracles. Are you hoping for one?"

Jeff dropped his head and began running his hands through his hair, struggling to find an answer. It was apparent that he was a broken man.

Lifting his head, he said, "Watching the service—it was an atmosphere filled with love. First, the story of the Christmas child, then Tina's song, and Robin …" He stopped. His eyes were brimming with tears. "I couldn't believe all the families. I envied them."

"Christmas is a family time," Chris added.

"When Robin and Tina walked out of the church, I felt such guilt, yet I wished I walked out with them. I didn't want her to live, and there she was. Could they ever forgive me?" He lowered his head and sobbed.

Chris needed to give him a few minutes. He sent a quick text to Kristen saying he had an urgent situation and would be a little late. He added that he might be bringing someone home with him.

After several minutes, Chris laid his hand on Jeff's shoulder.

"You will need to forgive yourself, but that will take time. God has brought you here for a reason, and in time you *will* understand. You've taken the first steps. I can see this hasn't been easy for you."

"I left my home, my unborn child, and the only woman I ever loved. I know Tina is mine. I can feel it. I thought leaving would change my life for the better. The perfect life I was looking for turned out to be miserable, and I never did find happiness."

"It's often hard to understand God's ways, but he does know what's best. You can't go back and change the past, but God can help you change what's ahead. Would you like me to pray with you?"

Jeff nodded his head and dropped to his knees. Chris placed his hand on his shoulder again. "Heavenly Father, thank you for bringing Jeff here tonight of all nights. I lift him up and bring his burdens to you. Help him to feel your forgiveness for past mistakes and then your unconditional love. Fill him with hope and peace in his life in the days ahead. Show him the way he should go. Thank you for the blessing this family with Tina. I pray for your will to be done in this situation. Thank you, Jesus, for being our light. We wait patiently and confidently for direction from you. You, Lord, are our strength. Bless Jeff this Christmas season."

"What are your plans for the holiday, Jeff?"

"I don't have any," Jeff responded.

"No family or friends?" Chris asked.

"It's all complicated and a messed-up story, but I don't want to keep your family waiting."

"Jeff, God brought you here to this place now for a reason. I trust him totally, and I never tire of doing my part in his plans. So my guess is you are meant to be part of my family's Christmas Eve. You are welcome to come home with me. Warning—my children are excited."

"Are you sure? I don't want to impose."

"Believe me, there is enough food for an army. The members of our congregation love to drop food off. Plus, my wife had a cookie-baking and -decorating marathon with the kids and Tina several times."

"My Tina?" Jeff asked.

"Why, yes. Tina stayed with us while Robin was in the hospital, and now the kids are close."

"Did I just say *my*?"

"You did. Was it an awkward feeling?"

"No—natural. The moment I saw her, I felt a connection."

Chris looked over at the nativity. *Yes, Lord, I think he is receiving your message. More miracles to come, I'm sure. I love this work, Lord.*

"We should go." Chris finished locking up, and they went to their cars.

Chris noticed Jeff's Florida plates. He had made quite a journey to get here. It looked like when he left New York State, he had gone as far away as he could.

CHAPTER 19

Robin stood over Tina's bed, watching her sleep. Such innocence, such love and sweetness. How was that possible? She sat in the rocking chair next to the bed and closed her eyes. The last ten years was not how she envisioned her life would be. Despite all the pain and struggle, her life was perfect.

Tears streaked down her cheeks when she thought back to the church program. Tina made her so proud.

Thank you, Lord, for my perfect family. Your ways are not my ways, but I've trusted you all these years, and I'm going to trust you now. I thank you for each day with Tina. We made so many memories. I never imagined such peace and happiness could come through a child, but you did.

Thank you for never leaving us alone and for all those times with Dad. Dad, I hope you were watching tonight. She brought her Christmas gift to you and Jesus in heaven tonight.

I am looking forward to what is to come, Lord. Lead us. In Jesus's name I pray. Amen.

When she reached for the tissues on the nightstand, she noticed the slightly opened drawer. This room had been her room, and she had also used it when she visited with Jeff. Opening the drawer quietly, she saw her framed wedding picture, which she thought her mom must have tucked it in the drawer. Opening the drawer a little more, she saw a second empty frame. *Did Dad take the picture? Mom? Tina? No, it couldn't be Tina.* She never knew her father or ever asked about her father. Robin took both frames from the drawer and closed it.

She stood over Tina again. This child had been full of surprises her whole life. She couldn't understand about her father. The only father she knew was her heavenly Father.

Robin went back down to the family room. Betty sat watching *It's a Wonderful Life*.

"I always loved that movie. *Scrooge* is coming on. Do you want to watch it?"

"Thanks, maybe in a little bit."

"Are you feeling all right?" Betty asked.

"I'm not quite back to normal, but close. Mom, I'm puzzled about something."

Betty looked alarmed. "What did I do?"

"Nothing. There were some pictures in Tina's nightstand drawer. Did both frames contain pictures?"

"In my haste to get the room ready, I stuffed them in there. There weren't any empty frames."

"So this was after Dad died?"

"Yes. You don't think …"

Robin shrugged her shoulders and said, "Only God knows. I can't worry about it now. I'm going to wrap a few things."

"I thought we wrapped them all. Do you need help?"

"Kristen and Marcy helped me sneak some shopping in, and I managed to hide some things from even you."

Betty laughed. "I can't wait until tomorrow. Remember, there are all those gift bags in the office. It saves time."

"I love those bags—as long as you won't peek."

"Promise," Betty replied. She couldn't imagine another gift. Her heart was filled with so much joy already.

Robin went upstairs and found the bags. It didn't take long, and soon she was laying on the couch in time to see Scrooge receive his first ghost's visit.

Kristen greeted Jeff and Chris at the door.

"Welcome. I am afraid it is a little chaotic here. I'm Kristen. This is Chloe and Robbie."

Chris took Jeff's coat and led him into the family room. The room was cozy, with a beautifully decorated tree near the window with a pile of wrapped presents underneath.

"Jeff, make yourself comfortable while Kristen and I help settle these two into bed. This is the big night."

Waiting, Jeff noticed a large package with Tina's name on it under the tree. A few packages looked like they had been wrapped by a child. Small index card labels with hand-drawn pictures on them labeled each one.

Jeff recognized the similarity to the picture on the screen during the service. He picked up a package to take a closer look.

"Quite an artist too," Chris said from behind him.

"Are you saying Tina did this?" Jeff asked.

"Yes, she loves to draw and spends a lot of time doing it."

"That was her picture on the screen tonight?"

"Yes. Her participation helped our service to be one of the best Christmas Eve services we've held. She has made an impact here at Limestone Presbyterian."

"I'm so confused. I never realized Down syndrome children were so capable. I never expected the singing either. No one recognizes her handicap."

"God created every person, and each is unique. We need to embrace the differences."

"But don't you think it ruined Robin's life in some way?" Jeff asked.

"Jeff, you haven't been around Robin for some time. I can't explain her life in Rochester. One thing I know to be true is her life is simple and complete, without material possessions."

"But how?"

"All things are possible with God. Robin's strong faith helped her endure the tough times. Look at the Christmas story. Our Lord was brought into the world in a manger. He was a King born in humble beginnings."

"I often wondered about Robin," Jeff said.

"How about your life? Did you find happiness and prosperity?" Chris asked.

"I spent my happiest times with Robin. I've made lots of money but never found real happiness. Robin and I had plans to go places."

"God's plans for a person's life are greater than our own. Robin understands and accepts his will for her life."

"But she can't own much. How could she provide as a single mom?"

"Robin will need to answer your questions," Chris said.

"Maybe Nate helped. He was a great man. I was surprised to see Betty with Robin. Betty supported an abortion too," Jeff said.

"She did, and I think if you talked to Betty, you would find her a different person now. Perhaps you made the wrong choice?"

"My job pays well, and I live in a great place with everything I could want," Jeff said.

"Everything?" Chris asked. "What about family or love?"

"My family loves me, and they live in Florida too."

"But you are not there on Christmas, nor do you plan to be. How about marriage?"

"Work and traveling make relationships hard. My climb up the corporate ladder involved some meaningless liaisons. Once I became CEO of my company, a goal I worked hard for, I still wasn't happy."

"Something missing—huh?"

"Thing is, I just felt I was trying to buy something to fill a void," Jeff said.

"Buy?"

"You know, dinners, parties, travel, and clubs. The list goes on and on."

"No, I guess I don't. I prefer a life of simplicity."

"Things are different here. My grandparents lived near here. My parents provided the basics, but I dreamed."

"Robin shared happy childhood memories here."

"And now Tina lives here."

"Let's focus on Christmas. Kristen's coming in to join us. You are welcome to stay in our guest room. The night's early though, and I'm warning you, we have a tradition of watching *It's a Wonderful Life*. Care to join me with my wife?"

"I think I would," Jeff said. "And thanks for listening."

"Glad you're here. I'll go find some Christmas goodies and Kristen."

Jeff sat down on the sofa and continued staring at those hand-decorated packages under the tree.

CHAPTER 20

Jeff woke refreshed but disoriented. He could smell coffee and saw the early hour on the clock. It took him a moment to register that he wasn't dreaming and Christmas morning had arrived.

Last night's discovery of being a father of a child he never even met stirred unfamiliar feelings. The family movie helped with the realization that choices lead to consequences that affect many people. His past decisions had been selfish.

Hurriedly he dressed and went downstairs. Torn wrapping paper surrounded Chloe and Robbie, and their excitement on Christmas morning bought back his own childhood memories. Suddenly, his thoughts went to Tina. What would Christmas morning be like with her?

"Mr. Anderson, would you like to open your present?" Robbie asked. The question interrupted his thoughts and also surprised him.

"Mine? Oh no, I wouldn't have a present here," he answered.

"But you do. It must be from Santa."

Chris winked at him, and Robbie handed him a package. Opening it, he found a Bible inside.

"Wow, Santa must have known I didn't own one. This is great," he said, looking at Chloe and Robbie.

"Santa always brings the best things. Right, Dad?" Chloe asked.

"That's right, sweetie."

"We'll be back shortly. Make yourself comfortable," Chris said.

Jeff sat watching the children play with their presents. Tina's unwrapped, decorated packages remained under the tree. He was about to ask about them when the doorbell rang.

"Jeff, would you mind opening the door? We've got our hands full in the kitchen," Chris yelled out.

The children were busy playing with their new gifts.

To his surprise, Tina stood there smiling.

"Hey, Merry Christmas. I'm Tina."

"I'm ... I'm a friend of the family. Come in."

"Tina, Merry Christmas. Come in and look at the cool stuff we got," Robbie said.

"Sorry, Mr. Anderson, she's just got to see what we got her," Chloe said, pulling Tina into the room before Jeff could say anything else.

Jeff was about to close the door when a woman he recognized from church came up the walk.

"Hi, I'm Molly. Robin is still recovering from her accident, so I offered to bring Tina over. Are you a friend of the family?" she asked.

"Yes, a friend. I'm Jeff," he said. By now he was a friend. Anyway, he felt like they cared.

The squeals coming from the family room quickly drew their attention.

Tina stood in front of an easel and held pastel crayons. She was ecstatic. The joy in the faces of the children giving her the gift amazed Jeff.

Chloe and Robbie opened the gifts Tina had made. Beautifully framed and illustrated Bible verses delighted the children.

How often had he tried to buy the "perfect" gift for someone? Most were hastily bought, thoughtless gifts. Missing the whole point of Christmas filled him with more regrets.

"Kids, help pick up quickly before brunch. Remember, we are going to serve lunch at the homeless center today," Kristen said. She turned to Jeff and asked, "Can you stay for brunch? You are welcome to come to the center with us too. Unless you have plans?"

Plans—no, no plans. Christmas and no plans.

"Sure, why not?" he answered.

"Me too?" Tina asked.

"Molly, can you please call Robin and ask? I forgot to mention our plans to her," Chris said.

She nodded.

Brunch was wonderful with all homemade dishes and pastries. His Christmases spent in restaurants now seemed artificial. *Why did this feel so right?*

The kids didn't notice Jeff watching as they ate. Tina's speech impairments didn't impede their conversations. Maybe he was the one with a mental abnormality. The rest of the world looked past her differences.

"Chris, I'll help at the center, but I think I'm going to take off after that. I appreciate spending time here and you listening to me."

"I'm glad we talked about your difficult circumstances. Where will you go?" Chris asked.

"I don't know. I need some time to think and find my own answers," Jeff said.

"You might want to start with the Bible," Chris said.

Jeff chuckled. "I somehow thought you would suggest that."

Tina and Molly came in the door about three o'clock. Molly asked to talk with Robin for a few minutes. Although Robin felt much better, she still tired easily partly due to Christmas busyness. Doctor Edwards prescribed physical therapy after the holiday.

Betty was busy getting dinner. Much of the food had been donated by church members, but Betty liked to add her own touches. She looked so happy. Molly found still found it difficult to believe how hardhearted she had been when they'd met a few short weeks ago. Her change was another example of God's power to fix an impossible situation.

Tina hung up her coat and gave Betty a big hug. Tina began sharing what happened at the center and showed Betty the easel. Molly went into the family room.

Robin laid on the couch watching Christmas movies.

"How are you?" Molly asked.

"Pretty good. Not quite ready for the Olympics, but I'm getting better every day. Everyone has been so kind and helpful," she said.

Tina walked in, gave her mom a kiss, and went upstairs.

"Robin, first I want to tell you how much you and Tina touched so many lives. This Christmas brought people together despite their personal problems," Molly said.

"Your words are kind, and we do feel accepted here. Tell me, how did the lunch at the center go? I'm sorry I left you short on help, but my doctor insisted I need more rest."

"Things went well. I love working there on Christmas Day. Tina was so cute and helpful. She sang again, and those homeless people—some people cried. They loved her."

"God did surprise me when I first heard her voice. Did you—"

Molly interrupted, "Sorry, before I forget—Chris brought an extra volunteer to fill your spot. He stayed with his family last night, and he fascinated Tina. She acted like she had known him a long time."

"Who was he? Does he go to our church?"

Molly liked hearing her say our church. "No, I met him at Chris's house this morning. He didn't look like a family member. Chris mentioned his family couldn't come this year. His name was Jeff. We didn't have much of a chance to talk at the center or at the house."

Robin's face went pale. "Are you sure he wasn't a relative?"

"Yes. Kristen's and Chris's family visited several times over the years. I've never met him."

Tina came back downstairs before Robin could ask more. She was holding a package and smiling.

"For you, Momma. Merry Christmas!" she said, handing the package to Robin.

Robin wanted to ask more questions, but she hesitated with Tina there. Betty came in and saw the package.

"Robin, you need to open that. I don't know what's in there. Tina kept it a secret from me too. I could hear her all the way in the kitchen."

"Open it please, Momma," Tina urged.

Robin's face changed to shock as she unwrapped the missing picture of Jeff and her. Tina had added herself to the picture with crayon and also added a label: Momma, Daddy, Tina.

Molly and Betty looked on, focusing on Robin's face.

Robin quickly composed herself. "Oh, Tina, Momma loves it so much. Why don't you give me a big hug?"

As Tina hugged her, Betty and Molly looked at the picture. Molly whispered something to Betty.

"Wow, Tina. You are such an artist! Now Momma needs some rest, and I need your help in the kitchen. Would you help me?" Betty asked.

"Sure," she said but looked into Robin's eyes for assurance.

"Yes, honey, Grandma is right. Thank you for my beautiful gift."

Tina went off to the kitchen with Betty. Tears started running down Robin's cheeks. That picture brought back so many memories. Lost dreams, betrayal, and broken promises. *Why now, God?*

Robin looked at Molly, "Did you say that fellow at Chris's house was called Jeff? Look at this picture—is this the man with Chris today?"

Molly took the picture from her hands. Clearly the picture was Robin and Jeff when they were much younger. "That's him; I'm certain. He looks older and like he's been through a lot, but I recognize him."

"How can this be? Why would he be here after ten years?"

"He appeared to be a nice guy, and Tina just loved—" She stopped. "They immediately connected, and I can't explain why."

"Why would God let this happen? We are just starting to build a relationship with my mother. I don't understand."

"Robin, you understand God's plans or purposes may be different than ours. You trust God, don't you?"

"God is the only reason I made it through these years. I loved Jeff, but he left me when I needed him the most."

"God's ways aren't our ways. He chooses the path, not us."

"Molly, I don't think I want him back in my life. He doesn't deserve to be here."

"Robin, we don't deserve God's mercy either, but he gives it whether we deserve it or not. He wants us to do the same."

"But Molly, he said he could never be the father of what he called a challenged child. He didn't want her."

"All I can say is he watched Tina with loving eyes."

"I've never talked to her about him."

"I think she sensed a bond. She gives love the way God gives it—unconditionally."

"I can't do this!" Robin cried.

"No, you can't, but God can help you. Let's pray," she said.

Molly took Robin's hand and prayed.

Father God, thank you for your many blessings and love you have given us. Thank you for your Christmas gift of your Son and the gift of grace. We know that your grace is sufficient to get us through this time that we do not understand. We trust you to work things out for good, not evil. Be with Robin, and help her to cling to you alone and not dwell on the pain inside. Bless Jeff, and use these circumstances to bring glory to you and you alone. In Jesus's name we pray. Amen

"Serving at the center helps me appreciate how blessed I am. My family is waiting for me. We'll talk soon. God is good!"

"Thanks, Molly. Merry Christmas," Robin said.

CHAPTER 21

Robin could hear Tina and Betty in the kitchen. Living together no longer seemed awkward since Betty's disposition had changed. Robin looked at her gift from Tina. The day it was taken was a vivid memory, and she wondered if Tina had recognized Jeff was her dad. Why was he here?

So many questions that wouldn't be answered today. Those old feelings of bitterness and resentment did not have a place in her heart again. The Christian community at her former church helped keep her accountable to not let negative emotions overpower her. Forgiveness is one of the hardest things she learned to do, but it really set her free to enjoy life.

More questions started running through her mind. What did Jeff say to Tina?

Robin just bowed her head. *Lord, forgive me for these anxious thoughts. I trust you and your wisdom. Thank you for this season. Help me focus on you.*

Her questions had to wait. Answers would come at the right time. Nothing was going to spoil Christmas.

"Momma, come and look at the table."

Robin's surprise delighted Tina. Her mother's china looked beautiful on silver chargers.

"Mom, this table is so beautiful! You two have been busy this afternoon."

Special Christmas candlesticks surrounded the lovely boxwood centerpiece decorated with silver and mauve to match the dining room. Even the napkin rings matched the dishes and chargers.

"Momma, sit," Tina urged, pointing to a spot.

There were four place settings with place cards.

"Who's joining us?" Robin asked.

"J," Tina answered.

Robin looked over at her mom, but Betty shrugged her shoulders.

"Honey, please sit down, and we will bring the food in."

Tina went out to the kitchen.

"Robin, I've got to help her. She is so excited about what we're having. Tina and I made a special dessert."

Betty helped Tina bring in a food cart filled with food. They both looked so cute in their matching Santa aprons. She wished her dad had been there to see this.

"Let's pray," Robin said.

"Me, Momma, please," Tina pleaded.

"Sweetie, you go ahead."

"Thank you, Jesus, for Christmas, Momma, Grandma, Father Chris, Kristen, Chloe, Robbie, Molly, and all my friends." She paused. "Thank you for J too. Bless our food. *Amen.*"

Betty's apprehensive look confirmed she was not aware of who J was, and she immediately turned a Christmas CD on. When their plates were filled, Tina changed the conversation to the center. Betty was adjusted to Tina's slight speech impediments, and she now conversed with ease and genuine interest.

Robin's fatigue returned, and she was about to get up when Tina said, "Momma, back in a minute."

Betty followed her into the kitchen.

The place card with J left Robin feeling unsettled. Her thoughts wandered back to Jeff. What would she say if he stopped by?

The lights in the dining room went out as Betty walked in with a birthday cake. Tina sang Happy Birthday to Jesus. Robin let out an audible sigh. *She meant J for Jesus. How sweet!*

The cake was beautiful, and Tina clearly had helped with the decorating. Betty's skill with cakes came from years of cake-decorating classes.

The four candles on the cake flickered slightly.

"Who is going to blow out the candles and make a wish?" Robin asked, knowing who would.

"Me," Tina responded quickly.

Robin and Betty watched as she blew all the candles out. She then closed her eyes.

"Tina, are you wishing?" Robin asked.

"I sent a wish to Jesus," she said with a big smile on her face.

"Is that place for Jesus too?" Robin asked.

"No," Tina responded as she took the candles off the cake.

"Tina, come over here and help me cut this cake," Betty said.

Anxious thoughts came over Robin. *Lord, does she mean Jeff? I don't know if I can do this. Help me. Protect her.*

A peace came over Robin, and she looked around the table. With God all things were possible.

Ten years ago, she had prayed the same prayer. The Lord is near to the brokenhearted and sends protection. He moves mountains, like he did between Betty and Tina.

"Tina, you and Grandma are such great decorators. Jesus is probably looking down right now, and he's so happy."

Tina laughed. Robin saw her hands covered with frosting.

"Wait until your birthday. We've got plans, don't we, Tina?"

"Another surprise, Momma."

"Can't wait to see your next masterpiece!"

They all sat laughing and eating as Betty described the mess in the kitchen.

Jeff left the homeless center and followed the signs to Interstate 86. He instinctively took the Rochester exit, although his mind was cluttered with thoughts of the day. Conversations with Tina today made him wonder if she knew. Was he running away again? When he got to Henrietta, he took the exit to the Fagan Inn Express.

The lobby bustled with people loaded down with packages. A beautifully decorated tree stood in the center of the lobby, and he stood admiring it. The face of little angel on top reminded him of Tina when she sang on Christmas Eve. She not only played the part of an angel, but she sang like one too.

"Sir, can I help you?" he heard a voice interrupt his mindful wanderings.

Jeff looked at the smiling receptionist. *If only you could help*, he thought.

"I would like a room if you have one. Christmas is probably your busiest time," he said.

"We're not usually all booked on Christmas. Most people like to stay with relatives during the holidays. How about you—family in the area?" she asked.

"No, no family," he answered.

"I'm checking for a room," she said with a flushed face. "I've found a nice one. After you are settled in, you can come back down and enjoy our holiday buffet. The best around, I promise. Room service can also deliver a plate to your room if you prefer."

"Sure, sounds good. I'll let you know," he responded.

She handed him a room key—room 1015. He just stared at the numbers.

"Is there some problem, sir? The only room left is on the top floor," she asked.

"Problem? No. Sorry, I'll check back about dinner."

He grabbed his bag and headed toward the elevator. Robin's birthday was October 15—a date still circled on every calendar.

The elevator arrived quickly. The top floor wouldn't be as noisy, and he typically preferred quiet. Today Chris's house and the center were anything but quiet, and he didn't mind at all.

Once in his room, his thoughts went back to Robin. Sitting on the bed the emptiness of the room reminded him he was alone in a hotel room on Christmas. His window overlooked the city with sparkling Christmas lights.

The bed looked inviting. He laid down, and with closed eyes, he thought about Robin. She had always loved Christmas, and even when they had little money, she made it special with lights, cookies, music, and a nativity. One Christmas they had to eat pizza because they couldn't afford the gas to go home, but she made that memorable. Christmas had always been about joy for her, never gifts. The same joy had been on her face at the church last night.

His cell phone's ring startled him, and he recognized his mom's number. Another Christmas away from them.

"Merry Christmas, Mom," he said as cheerfully as possible.

"Hello, son, and Merry Christmas to you too. We were hoping to see you this year. I guess your work schedule kept you away again?" she asked.

"Truthfully, no, Mom. I'm in a hotel in Rochester."

The phone went dead; he had forgotten to charge it. Just as well. He didn't want to explain any of this to his parents. They had never wanted an abortion and wanted him to think carefully about leaving Robin. They didn't like his choices but always gave their love unconditionally. While he appreciated their support, the guilt made him avoid being around them.

As he opened his suitcase to get a change of clothes out, he picked up his new Bible, which was on top. Looking closely, he noticed his name was imprinted on the cover. How? In all the rush of the morning, he hadn't seen his name.

A bookmark made by a child was placed on Mark 10:15. It said, "Jesus loves you" and he recognized Tina's artwork. They were the same numbers for Robin's birthday.

Overcome by thoughts replaying in his mind, he cried out, "Oh, God, what do you want from me? I understand. I messed up."

How could God love him after the pain he had caused everyone? Then a real revelation came to him. How did she raise her alone? She never contacted him for anything. He never contributed a dime. Did that make him a deadbeat dad?

Like in Chris's office, he unknowingly fell to his knees. *I don't even know what faith is, God, or about the love of Jesus. Tina does. She has love for everyone. At the center she served the homeless people with love. I saw it at the church when she sang on Christmas Eve. God, do you think she could love me? I need your help. I am so lost here. Help me to be a better man and father, if it's not too late. I'm desperate here. Help.*

When a knock at the door interrupted, he realized he was on his knees.

The receptionist stood with a plate full of food when he answered. "The buffet shuts down at seven so the cook can go home to his family. I didn't want you to miss out, so I brought you a plate."

"Wow, thanks. How much do I owe you?" he asked.

"Nothing at all. The manager is a Christian, and when he observed your out-of-state plates, he insisted."

"Thanks, I appreciate this. Merry Christmas!"

"Merry Christmas to you too. If you are a Christian, we have a Christmas CD in the drawer next to the bed."

He thanked her again and placed the food on the small table. Then he put the CD in the player.

Reaching for his fork, he heard "Silent Night" begin to play.

CHAPTER 22

The alarm on his phone woke him. His fully charged phone already had ten messages, half of them from his mother. The clients could wait for now. This week was his vacation, and the messages probably were Christmas wishes anyways.

Another missed Christmas needed a bit of an explanation for his parents. He couldn't even think about it without coffee and a shower first. As he pulled the covers back, the Bible fell on the floor. He had fallen asleep reading the Bible beginning with Mark 10:15 and slept soundly for the first time since the video.

The bookmark fell out, along with Chris's business card. The card included his phone number and e-mail. He wondered why a pastor cared so much for a perfect stranger. The Christians at the hotel also went out of their way with extra kindness. Maybe it was the Christmas spirit. He ordered room service before he stepped into the shower.

Room service arrived soon after he finished dressing. Before he took his first bite, he thought about yesterday's brunch at Chris's house. Each person at the table said something they were thankful for. Yesterday he could only say thanks for hospitality. Today was different.

Lord, thank you for this food, but most of all, thank you for letting me spend time with my daughter at the center yesterday.

Breakfast was great, and he couldn't believe the excitement he felt. Something inside his heart longed to belong and feel again.

Jeff dialed his mom.

"Mom, sorry we got cut off yesterday. My phone died," he said.

"I'm just glad you're all right. We all missed you yesterday, especially your sister and her family. Your father and I aren't getting any younger," she added.

"I know. I'm sorry. I mean that."

"Son, what is going on? Why are you in New York?"

"Mom, there is something going on here, and I can't tell you now."

"Are you in trouble? We want to help. Remember, we love you no matter what."

"This is hard, Mom. You won't understand."

"I'm trying to, son, but you've seemed to shut us out since ... since you and Robin started having trouble. I've prayed—"

Jeff interrupted. "You prayed for me?"

"Of course, we've never stopped praying. We asked God to help you. Without Robin you've been lost. It has been so hard not knowing what happened to her or how to help with your difficult situation. You shut us out."

Jeff heard her voice start trembling with emotion. For ten years he had isolated himself from his loved ones.

"Mom, I don't have the words to explain now. But I can say, I love you and never meant to hurt anyone. I have made a lot of mistakes. I will visit in a few weeks. I promise I will."

"That would be wonderful! I am leaving the tree up until you visit."

Jeff laughed. "I guess I'd better come soon."

"Promise," she said.

"Promise. Mom, please keep praying for me. This will all make sense soon."

"See you soon," she said and hung up.

Jeff decided to go back to Lima right after a drive around their old neighborhood.

He packed his bags but decided to keep the Bible out as a reminder he wasn't alone.

Snow started falling lightly when he started down the interstate. In the few days he had spent in New York, he never noticed the snow on the ground. What else had he missed?

Again, his mind wandered to how Robin loved snowfalls. She never tired of playing in the snow and throwing snowballs at each other like little kids. Snow angels were the most fun. He pulled into the first rest stop and immediately got his wallet out. Digging deep into the hidden pocket, he pulled out a folded picture of Robin lying in the snow making a snow angel. Turning it over, he read his own handwriting: *My snow angel, my soul mate.*

The day he took the picture was one of the best days of his life. Robin always made life so refreshing and exciting. Love made everything easier. They played in the snow for hours that day—two adults who'd lost track of time. Grilled cheese, tomato soup, and hot chocolate always followed their snow frolics, as Robin called them. And he could talk to her about anything.

When Robin first found out she was pregnant, they couldn't contain their happiness. A few months later, the doctor found an abnormality, and given a family history (Robin's distant cousin) of Down syndrome, Robin underwent the suggested testing. Robin was adamant about not having an abortion because it would violate her Christian beliefs. He refused to sacrifice his happy future for such a child. What a mistake!

Looking up from the picture, he placed it on the Bible sitting on the passenger's seat. For the first time, he saw things differently and realized how callous he had been. An abortion ended a life. What did the Bible say about children?

He searched the index for verses about children. He realized all children were valued.

That Christmas Eve service had opened his eyes to his mistake. Robin had made the right choice. He was the one who had changed.

His life had been full of empty things and loneliness since losing his soul mate. He needed to understand God's perspective on the situation and his next steps. Chris was the only one able to help him find answers.

Chris arrived at his office a little later than usual. Marilyn usually took this week as vacation to be with her family. In the past, nothing urgent demanded attention the week after Christmas, which provided him the opportunity to reflect and make notes for next year.

A month ago, things at the church had been falling apart. With low attendance and declining donations, Molly thought the Christmas children's program would need to be canceled. God's intervention and provision resolved each one of the pressing problems and revived the congregation's hope for their future.

The luncheon at the homeless center provided meals for many families. The upbeat atmosphere brought joy to many discouraged families. When Tina sang some Christmas songs, everyone joined in whether they could sing or not. It was refreshing. Perhaps he would suggest a spring concert to raise some funds for the center.

Tina didn't seem to be afraid of serving or even being around homeless people. She didn't see how needy they were.

Jeff's presence at lunch made things uncomfortable but helped take Jeff's mind off his issues. Chris had seen the regret in his eyes each time he looked at Tina. When she smiled at him, his eyes lit up. How often people make mistakes that never get fixed because of pride. Would pride stand in his way?

Chris watched Betty pull into the church parking lot. She was alone. He unlocked the door for her.

"Good morning, Betty. Please come in," he said.

"Hi, Pastor. I'm hoping I can take a few minutes of your time to talk about a problem."

"Sure, let's go to my office. Things are a little quiet around here today, and Marilyn is out. How was your holiday, Betty?" he asked.

"Pastor, I must admit it was enjoyable. I miss Nate so much, but Tina and Robin kept me busy."

"I imagine it would be difficult without him."

"Those scrapbooks he made are filled with photos, so I always have a piece of him with me."

"That's great. What about Robin?"

"She is still recovering from the bruises and a few headaches. I think she will get back to work soon."

"I'm sure she'll need the money," Chris added.

"Actually, with Nate's smart investing, he saved enough to provide for us all. Robin's not aware of how he saved and will probably work because she does love her career."

"Then what is the problem?"

"I don't know what to do about Tina's father, Jeff," she said.

"What do you mean?" he asked.

"Tina knows Jeff is her father."

"Are you sure?"

"She set a place at our table yesterday for him. She told me it was for him."

"Is Robin aware of this?"

"No. But Molly told her about the center and seeing him at your house."

"Kristen and I are sorry we didn't warn her. When he approached me after the service, we talked. He didn't have a place to go, and I invited him to stay at our home. I forgot Tina was coming over in the morning."

"I don't blame you. Nate told her about Jeff before he died."

"And you know this because …?"

"Nate wrote two letters to go with the books. The second letter was in last one. He asked me to forgive and welcome Jeff back into the family. For over ten years he's been praying for reconciliation. He also gave Tina a picture of them and told her to keep praying for her father to find them."

"Do you think they can be reconciled after so long?"

"If Robin can forgive this foolish, hardhearted old woman, I think she will forgive the love of her life."

"Ten years is a long time."

"My concern now is how do I help with Jeff?" Betty asked.

"For starters, we will pray for your strength to able tell her about the letter. Then give her time to process and pray. Her respect for her dad's decisions in the past will help."

"Thank you!"

They bowed their heads and prayed.

"Betty, here is my card. If you need my help, do not be afraid to call or text. God has gotten you this far; he will not leave you now," he said. He walked her out to the door.

The remarkable changes in Betty could only be divine. *Lord, you are up to something.*

CHAPTER 23

Jeff pulled into the almost-empty church parking lot just as Betty entered the building. *Not a good time*, he thought. He decided to find a coffee shop to pass some time.

Two blocks away he spotted the Lima Bookstore/Cafe. The town had grown since the last time he had stayed with Betty and Nate but not as rushed as in Fort Lauderdale—another welcome change.

The bookstore was quaint, and although the selections were limited, he found a book on Down syndrome. With a latte and book in hand, he found a table in the back and began to read. He was unaware that there had been dramatic improvements in the health and quality of life for people with Down syndrome. The change in life expectancies from an average of twenty-five to almost sixty years astonished him. He stopped reading and decided on another coffee. Kristen was ahead of him.

"Kristen, I wanted to say thank you again for Christmas Eve and Christmas morning. You made me feel like part of your family."

"Our pleasure. I didn't expect to see you today. Weren't you headed out of town to visit some relatives in Rochester?" she asked.

"I did go to Rochester, but not to visit anyone. Robin and I used to live there. I don't even know why I went there."

"Sorry you felt you had to leave. Christmas day does get rather crazy," she said.

"I intruded. Please don't apologize. Can I buy you a cup of coffee?" he asked.

"Sure, why not?" she said. They ordered and walked over to Jeff's table.

"I see you are doing some research. The newspaper recently did a feature on it. The quality of life has improved for children because of research and studies," she said.

"This book mentioned some studies," he said.

"Do you mind if I ask you a question, Jeff?"

"You can ask. I can't guarantee I'll answer," he said.

"When Robin found out about your baby, what did you envision?"

"Please don't judge me when I explain. I was so young and unprepared. I anticipated a life burdened by a needy child."

"That's an honest answer. What did Robin think?" she asked.

"Robin was ecstatic about her pregnancy until she the prenatal test results. Considering an abortion angered her," he said.

"When did she decide not to?"

"I can't answer," he answered.

"Why not?"

"Kristen, we fought for a couple of weeks. Her mom wanted to her to abort too. Robin wouldn't listen to our reasons. Then the job offer from Florida we waited for came through before she decided. After the abortion, I wanted to start a new life in Florida."

"And she said no to everything?"

"Yes, and I told her she could ruin her life, but I wasn't ruining mine. I asked for a divorce."

"You never called her or anything?"

Jeff paused for a moment. "I filed the papers and called her to tell her they were coming."

"Robin must have been devastated. She never reached out?"

"No. My parents moved too. I was so mad that I never told her where to reach me."

"You've never wondered about her?"

"I loved Robin. I mean I still love her. I messed up big time."

"But you never checked?"

"I am ashamed to say no. I was selfish and bitter because she didn't support my dream job."

"And now?"

"These past few days gave me a glimpse of the life as it could have been, and I regret I am on the outside looking in. They are obviously happy."

"They are, despite the struggles. Do you deserve to be happy?" she asked.

"I'm not proud of my actions. Watching how the homeless people accepted Tina helped reinforce my guilt."

Kristen could tell his spirit was crushed. "Don't you think you're being hard on yourself?" she asked.

"How do I move on now?"

"The only way to heal would be through the true healer. God is already changing your heart."

"I read about forgiveness in the Bible."

"Believe me, Jeff, he loves you and does not think less of you because of the circumstances. You were so young. Ask for forgiveness, and he will give it to you. Then talk to Robin. Last, forgive yourself."

"That sounds so simple," he said.

"Healing from ten years of pain takes time. Anger takes a lot of power away from you and keeps the pain alive. God wants you to give your burdens to him through prayer."

"What about Tina? Will she forgive me?" he asked.

"That little girl is the most loving child I know. Yesterday she sensed something about you and will give you nothing but love. Take this to the Lord. He can do what we can't. Pray."

Kristen took Jeff's hand as she started to pray quietly.

"Thank you, Kristen. A week ago I never would envision me sitting in a cafe praying. It helped."

"My pleasure, Jeff. By the way, you will find it helpful to read the Bible each day."

"I actually fell asleep reading it last night."

"Good. Keep reading. My family is waiting, so I need to go. Bye," she said, getting up. She walked to her car smiling. *God, I sense your healing touch. Thank you, Lord.*

Betty wasn't sure how her talk with Robin would go. Though Robin had forgiven her, she feared telling Robin about Jeff would put another barrier between them. Since she had unwrapped Tina's present yesterday, Robin refused to talk about Jeff.

The light snowfall and the Christmas decorations made the town so picturesque. Appreciating simple things like driving down a snow-covered street pleased her. Her daily prayers and renewed faith changed her outlook on life.

Betty took a detour from her usual route home to stop by the cemetery. Holiday preparations interrupted her usual daily visits to Nate's grave, and she needed to talk to him even if he couldn't answer.

The snow falling on newly placed headstone covered his name. Brushing the snow off with her gloves, she found a handwritten note placed by the stone. Betty recognized Tina's writing. The snow had blurred the marker message slightly, but she could still read it:

Thank you, Poppy.

I came, and he loves me.

The picture showed Tina sending hearts and music notes to heaven and an angel in the sky labeled Poppy.

How did Tina get that note here and when? Betty wondered.

Betty felt a little alarmed, but she still took a few moments to talk to Nate. "Nate, I miss you so much. I wish I hadn't been a fool for so long and missed out on your times with Tina. She is so beautiful. Thank you for the memory books. Looks like you took care of my girls all along. They miss you too. I'm going home to start my own memory book. First, I have to talk with Robin about Jeff. He's here, but I guess you already know. If you're watching down on us, please bless us and help me talk to Robin. Jeff needs our forgiveness too. I love you, sweetie, and I wish you were still here so you could enjoy our family together. Forgive me. I'm so sorry. I will be back soon. I need to check on Tina."

Betty thought she sensed his presence for a moment, but maybe it was just wishful thinking.

The wind picked up, and the snow started falling a little heavier. *Time to head home. We don't need another car accident,* she thought. She noticed two sets of footprints leading away from Nate's headstone. One set was very large and the other much smaller. *Strange—who else was here today?* First she thought Robin had brought Tina while she was with Chris, but those footprints were *not* Robin's.

CHAPTER 24

With coffee in hand, Robin stood at the kitchen window watching the snow piling up. She fondly remembered childhood memories of waiting for her dad to take her out to play in the snow. The trees glistened and bowed with the heaviness of the accumulating snow. *Tina is going to love to play out there*, she thought. Christmas Eve and Christmas day were exhausting for them all. Tina and Betty had not come down yet.

God's protection prevailed these past few weeks. *Glory and praise to you, Lord, for all you have blessed us with this Christmas. Thanks for turning things around and bringing my family together.*

Her prayer stopped when she saw Jeff walking up to the back door. She froze. He didn't notice her in the window.

Her hands began to tremble, and she set the cup down. His hand hesitated before knocking, and his eyes lingered for a moment to look toward the backyard—the same backyard where he had proposed all those years ago when she was home on college break. As he stood staring, she could see his eyes filled with tears. Ten years and not a word. Why now, and how did he know she was here? Better yet, did Tina understand he was the same man in the picture?

The knock interrupted her thoughts. She answered quickly, hoping Tina would not be awakened by the sound.

"Jeff? What are you doing here? How did you know where I lived now?" she asked.

"Hello, Robin. I need to talk to you."

"Need to talk? Remember, you ended our marriage ten years ago because you were on your way to the top and I was holding you back. A little late to talk, don't you think?" she said, starting to close the door.

"What about Tina?" he asked.

Robin stood holding the door. Overcome with panic, she started to feel short of breath. The last thing she remembered was thinking, *Father, help me.*

When she opened her eyes, she was being held by Jeff.

"Are you all right? Do I need to call the doctor? Let me get you some water," he said, helping her up to a chair.

He went to the sink and filled a glass with water. She slowly sipped it and regained her composure.

"I'm fine. Really, you can go."

"Robin, I came here to talk."

"Jeff, I don't think we have anything to say after this long. Our life is good here."

"You are right about what I did and said years ago. If I could take it back, I would. But I can't."

"Then why are you here?" she asked.

"To ask for your forgiveness for being so selfish. I made the biggest mistake of my life when I left you."

Those exact words were what she had longed to hear many years ago. So many nights spent praying he would come back and say them. Her breathing started to become erratic again. She sipped more water and closed her eyes. *Father, help me.* She took deep breaths. *Open your heart, child. Look into his eyes. See the regrets. Forgive.*

Eyes opened, she looked at his face. He had moved a chair closer to her and looked right in her eyes. She hadn't even noticed he had taken her hands into his. She recognized the pain in his eyes. His face was as worn and aged as Molly had described it. Did he mean what he was saying?

"Robin, I realize I am asking more than I have a right to ask. A day hasn't gone by that I don't think about you. I've had this big, empty hole in my heart. I *never* stopped loving you. Forgive me, please."

Wasn't forgiveness and grace the essence of the New Testament and the reason for the death of Jesus? It was the hardest thing to give when the pain cut so deep.

"As a Christian, I am called to forgive. For months after you left, I cried out to God every night. He gave me the strength to go on, but I still prayed for you to come back. When Tina was born, I promised God I would forgive you. Every day when I got up, I forgave you again until the pain waned. God's strength helped me move on, but I never forgot."

"Thanks for your honesty. I really don't deserve anything from you. Do you think Tina will forgive me?"

"Tina? I never told her a thing about you. The only father she knows is her heavenly Father."

Before Jeff responded, the front door opened and Betty's voice called out, "Robin, whose car with Florida plates is in the driveway? I couldn't pull in, and the snow is piling up."

They listened to the sound of her taking her boots off in the entranceway and waited in silence.

Betty stood in shock when entered the kitchen.

"Hello, Betty," he said.

"What are you doing here? Haven't you hurt her enough? I think you should leave."

"Mom, he will leave when we finish our conversation. We need closure. Tina still isn't up. Would you mind checking on her? Here, take some fruit juice and muffins up to her so we can talk here."

Betty looked confused. "Are you sure you want me to leave?"

"Yes, Mom. I am."

"Tina hasn't been down yet?" she asked Robin.

"No, she's probably exhausted from yesterday. Thanks for understanding, Mom."

Betty placed the breakfast on a small tray. Her eyes sent questioning looks to Robin and Jeff, but she didn't say a word.

With the sound of her footsteps on the stairs, Robin's attention went back to Jeff.

"Jeff, what do you want from me?" she asked.

They heard a crash from upstairs.

Jeff and Robin got up quickly. Jeff helped steady Robin as they went through the family room to the stairway.

Betty came down. "Tina's not upstairs," she said.

"Where is she?" Robin asked.

Jeff asked, "Could she be hiding somewhere? Is she in the bathroom?"

"Robin, she's *not* here. I put her coat right here on this coat rack last night. It is gone."

Panic filled them all as they saw the snow piling up out the front window.

Betty and Jeff kept watching Robin.

"I am not going to panic. God has always watched over us. I trust him." She took their hands and bowed her head.

Jeff said, "Let me."

He poured out his heart to God.

Jeff could feel Robin's hands shaking.

"Now what?" Jeff asked.

"Well, first I'm getting dressed. I'll be back down in a minute."

Jeff and Betty stood alone in the kitchen.

"You're thinking this is because of me, aren't you?" he asked.

"Let's focus on our little girl. I haven't been the best mother or grandmother either, so I'm not going to judge anyone. But I'll tell you this, if you came here to hurt either of them, you need to leave *now*!"

"I'm not going to ever hurt them, I promise."

"Good, because you'll need to deal with me if you do," Betty said.

"Understood."

Robin came into the family room all dressed for the snow. Memories of times they had spent in the snow flooded Jeff's mind, and he wondered if she was thinking the same thing. He changed his focus back to Tina.

"Where would she go or why? We didn't make plans with anyone to do anything today. Mom, do you remember seeing her coat before you left?"

"Hmm … When I left to see the pastor, it hung on the hook here in the foyer. I didn't wake you or Tina because you were both so exhausted last night."

"Mom, think. Can you think of anything she said or did yesterday while she was with you?"

"No, we had fun getting dinner ready, setting the table, and decorating that cake. She sang most of the time."

Jeff looked at Betty. "Did she say anything about meeting me?"

"You? I don't understand."

"Mom, Tina was at the homeless center yesterday with Chris and his family. Jeff was there too."

"How did …?"

"Molly told me. It's not like her to do something without telling me."

"Oh, no," Betty said, shaking her head.

"What is it, Mom?"

"I went to your father's grave after my visit with Chris this morning. Someone put one of Tina's pictures by the headstone. I thought Molly or Kristen stopped by yesterday on the way home."

"A picture?" Robin asked.

"It had a message too. It said, 'Thank you, Poppy. J came, and he loves me.'"

"J? Did she mean me?" Jeff asked.

"I'm not sure." Betty started crying.

"Mom, we'll find her. Don't worry."

"Honey, I have to tell you something about your father."

"Tell me what?"

"Apparently your father told her about Jeff. I found out yesterday when I read another letter in the last scrapbook, but I didn't realize it was true until she gave you the picture yesterday."

"So I am J?" Jeff asked. "And she said I loved her?"

Betty kept sobbing.

"Mom, you need to pull yourself together. We all do for Tina's sake. That snow is piling up, and she's out in it. Jeff, I can't drive yet, so would you mind driving my car?"

"Sure, but your car?"

"I'm sure your Florida car is not snow ready, right?" Robin asked.

"Gotcha."

"Mom, I need you to stay here in case she comes home. Also, please call Chris so he can call all the prayer warriors. Maybe some people can help search too. Then keep the phone open for calls."

"Robin, I just remembered something else."

"What is it?"

"At your father's grave, there were two sets of footprints going away from the stone and small dog prints. One set looked small, and another set looked large, like a man's size."

A chill went down Robin's spine, and she fell into Jeff.

"Robin, don't give up on your faith now. There are too many people in this town who know and love her. Someone will have information," Jeff said.

His words actually made sense to her. Tina had made so many friends at the center, at school, at church, and at the home where she worked. But if Jeff was here, whose tracks were those next to Tina's?

After Jeff moved his car to the side of the driveway, he backed Robin's car out of the garage and went in to get her.

"Let me help you," he said as she started down the snow-covered stairs. "You don't need another head injury."

"Seems like you know a lot about my life for someone who hasn't been around very long."

"We don't have time to get into that now, but Chris filled me in on recent developments."

"You're right, now is not the time."

Did he detect some hope for future conversations? He was a little encouraged.

"So, Robin, Tina kept things from you since your dad died?"

CHAPTER 25

"Last night she gave me a wrapped picture as a Christmas present. She had taken an old picture of you and me from an upstairs drawer. Then she added a picture of herself in the middle with markers."

"Robin, I promise, I didn't let on who I was."

"I noticed the missing picture on Christmas Eve, so the picture was missing before you met."

"How is that possible? I know she didn't see me at the church."

"You watched the Christmas Eve service?" Robin asked.

"It was pretty amazing."

"Jeff, I have a feeling my dad told her a lot about you."

"For now let's focus on our daughter, and we can catch up on the rest after we find her. I don't like her being out in this snow."

"Do you remember where the cemetery is?"

"I think so. This town hasn't changed that much. My grandparents are buried in it, remember?"

"I do."

"How did she get from the house to the cemetery?" he asked. "Wait a minute."

Jeff got out of the car and walked around the front of the house.

When he returned he said, "There are two sets of footprints leading from the door. Also, some dog tracks. They are almost covered now."

"Don't forget Mom came in the front."

"Robin," he said, laying his hand on her arm to steady her arm. "Two sets in addition to Betty's. The other prints are big, plus Tina's."

Robin sat back in her seat. "I think I might need to call the police."

Betty stayed busy making calls. She called Pastor Chris, and he said an e-mail would go out to the congregation. She sensed alarm in Chris's voice as he tried to assure her Tina would be found. He volunteered to make inquiries around town. Next she called Susan at the home where Robin worked but reached her voice mail.

In between calls, Betty kept looking out the window and worried more as the snow continued to fall. Her mind thought about Jeff and Robin. The urgency of the situation united them as two concerned parents looking for their lost child. Jeff's behavior had already convinced Betty he thought of Tina as his own. Would this emergency bring them back together for good? Was that Tina's plan? No—she was too innocent to plan something long term. God's plan was more like it.

Betty noticed Jeff get out of the car and go around to the front. At first she thought they forgot something, but he didn't come back into the house. They finally pulled out of the driveway.

She put the kettle on and sat down at the table. At any other time, this would be a beautiful snowy day. As the clock ticked, she was reminded of how dangerous the snow would be the longer Tina stayed missing.

Oh, little one, you are so full of surprises. She took one of the photo albums sitting on the nearby counter. All those memories she and Jeff had missed. Why didn't they take time to become more informed about Down syndrome instead of pressuring Robin? A small J with a heart in the corner appearing in the corner of the most recent pictures caught her attention. She went back to the beginning of the last album to take a closer look. On several pages Tina wrote, "Jesus loves me." No, this J meant Jeff. Tina never let on J meant Jeff.

Nate had told Tina about her father for a reason. He had said so in his letter, and here was the proof in the album. Again she said out loud this time, "What are you up to, my little one?"

She went into the family room and knelt.

Betty realized her prayer life was now all about relationship with Jesus, and she would never change back to the way life had been without him. No more shallow, rote prayers like her early Christian days. Tina had taught her to put Jesus in her heart, and there he would stay.

The whistling tea kettle brought her back to the kitchen. She anxiously waited by the phone. When it did ring, she jumped.

"Betty, Susan here. I had a message from you about Tina. Is this about Robin coming back to work, or is something wrong?"

"Susan, I'm afraid I have some bad news. Tina left the house this morning without telling us where she was going. We've found other footprints with hers."

"Betty, I'm so sorry. The snow is really accumulating. How is Robin doing with this?"

"She's out with Tina's father looking for her now."

"Tina's father? I didn't know he was around."

"Another one of our Christmas surprises. I'm afraid I'm going to let Robin fill you in later. I need to keep the line open. Ask everyone who is able to keep their eyes open for Tina."

"Betty, I'm going to ask some of my maintenance staff to go out immediately and help look. We all love that little girl. Let me know when you find her, if we don't find her first."

"Thank you, Susan."

Betty hung up, amazed at Susan's confidence and faith when she stated "when you find her."

CHAPTER 26

The snow was coming down heavier, making the roads slippery. Jeff had never thought snow was dangerous until now. His little girl being out in the storm frightened him. Life had changed so quickly. A few days ago his life didn't include a daughter and now … would he get to know her? Had something happened to her?

"Jeff!"

Robin's voice startled him.

"What?"

"You need to focus on the roads. You almost hit that car. I will look as you drive."

"Sorry, I haven't driven in this stuff in a long time," he answered. "There's the cemetery."

He pulled over and said, "Robin, it's slippery out there. We can't afford to have you fall. Stay here, please. Where is the grave?"

Robin pointed in the direction of the grave and agreed to stay put.

Jeff walked over to Nate's grave and the note laid against the headstone. Picking the note up, he held it like a fragile piece of glass. The wet snow had smeared the message, and only the J was legible. The snow covered most of the tracks. The depth of the bigger prints made it clear they belonged to an adult, which frightened him. Smaller animal prints could be seen all over the area. He took the note back to the car.

Robin recognized Tina's handwriting but couldn't fathom how she found this place by herself.

"The tracks are almost covered, but they are going that way," he said, pointing. "And I think the animal tracks are a dog. But those *big* tracks—do you think someone followed her?

"They are going toward the center. Let me follow up with the police and tell them what you found," she said.

"May I keep this?" Jeff asked.

Robin sensed how anxious he was. "Sure, but I'm sure Tina will make a new one if you ask her."

Such faith and determination, he thought. He felt her strength in God and wanted to believe. The snow started to fall more heavily, and Robin's strength would not last.

Lord, help me to be strong today, and most of all, protect our Tina please, he said in silence as he started down the road.

Chris called the prayer chain leader and put prayers in motion. Where could Tina be in this snow? Betty hadn't explained why Tina was missing, but she emphasized she might not be alone. Chris hoped Jeff was not responsible.

Chris called Kristen and asked her to make a few calls to their neighbors. Next he called Molly and asked that she call other churches to help pray and search. He worried Tina might become confused and lost in the snow. Robin kept her close to home, and she wasn't familiar with the town.

Chris went to his knees and prayed for her safety too. After nearly a half an hour, a thought came to him. Perhaps the men and women at the homeless center had seen her, or maybe they could help. They certainly knew and loved Tina in addition to knowing every alleyway and street in town. He quickly put on his coat and boots and went to the car.

The weather affected center attendance because many people wanted a warm place during snowstorms. Pete was getting the lunch line set up when Chris entered.

"Chris, I didn't expect you to come by today. Can I help you with something?" Pete asked.

"Pete, remember Tina from yesterday?"

"Remember? Everyone is still talking about it today. What a great Christmas lunch. What's wrong?"

"She is missing, and we are searching for her. The snow is really coming down, and she's out there someplace. Has she been here this morning?"

"No, not that I know of. Let me ask."

Pete stood on a chair in front of the lunch counter.

"Attention everyone—we need your help. Our little singing angel from yesterday is missing. Did anyone see her today?"

"I saw her over near the cemetery this morning. She was playing with a little black puppy," said Al.

"What time did you see her?" Pete asked.

"About eight fifteen this morning," he answered.

"Anyone else?"

"The little angel was playing with a little puppy near the park about nine thirty. I tried to talk to her, but when the puppy ran away, she followed," said Mary.

"Anyone else nearby?" Pete asked reluctantly.

"Joe followed her. I thought they were together," Mary answered.

"Pete, who is Joe?" Chris asked with alarm in his voice.

"Chris, Joe is harmless, a little odd, but you don't need to worry. He takes care of all the stray abandoned dogs and cats around and probably wanted to help catch the puppy."

"Any idea where they would head?" Chris asked.

A young woman came up to them. Chris recognized her from Christmas.

"Sir, that little one is safe with Joe. He knows where to go on a day like today. I can show you the way to where he takes the animals for shelter. She is probably there too."

"Great, but first let me make a quick call to Tina's mom. She's out looking for her." He went outside to make the call.

"Robin, I'm at the homeless center, and I do have a lead on where Tina might be. Why don't you come to the center and just wait for me? Pete will fill you in," Chris asked.

"We will head there now. The snow is getting heavy," she said.

"We'll find her," he said confidently.

Chris and Annie headed out to his snow-covered car. In the few minutes he had been inside, another inch of snow had accumulated.

CHAPTER 27

Jeff and Robin drove to the center as quickly as possible with the roads so snow covered. Robin kept massaging her temples intermittently while looking at her watch.

As they entered the center, they noticed everyone stood holding hands in a large circle, with Pete leading them in prayer.

"Lord, keep our little angel under your protection. She is precious, and we love her. Keep her sheltered and warm. In Jesus's name we pray. Amen."

The group remained in the circle with heads bowed long after he finished. After five more minutes of silent prayers, he finally said, "Let's get the hot lunch line ready. That little one will probably be cold and need a hot lunch."

Jeff watched as the group dispersed to various areas around the room. Many had tears running down their faces, and several positioned themselves by the window as though they were waiting for someone.

Pete came up to them. "Pastor Chris went out with Annie. We think Tina might be with Joe, who takes in stray animals on days like this. Have a seat. Would you like some coffee?"

Jeff and Ellen nodded and took seats at a table near the window.

Robin stared outside for a few minutes and then said, "She loves days like today. She and Dad would go out and make snow angels like—"

"Like you and I used to do?" he asked.

Robin wouldn't look at him.

"Being here helped me remember how much I miss those times,

Robin. Life has been so empty without you. No purpose. No fun. We had fun. Money can't buy times like that."

Robin understood his pain and loss because she missed those times too. But why didn't he come back sooner? Or was God testing her again?

"Look!" a young man shouted, pointing out the window.

Chris's car pulled up behind Robin's car. The steamed-up windows made it difficult to see the passengers.

"He's got our angel!" someone finally shouted out.

Robin felt such relief that she put her head in her hands and sobbed and thanked God.

"Momma, don't cry. I'm sorry," Tina said as she put her arms around her. Robin hugged her back.

"Tina, honey, you scared everyone. It's so cold out there and dangerous."

"Momma, Joe and I were taking care of Blackie. Blackie needed food."

"But Joe is a stranger. Remember what I said about strangers?"

"Robin, she does know him. She sang a few songs for him yesterday, and she met him a few weeks ago when she stopped in with Kristen," Pete said.

Tina shook her head in agreement.

"Well that doesn't mean he can take off with her to care for puppies. He had to know we would be worried," Robin snapped.

"Robin, I talked with Joe. Apparently that black puppy was near your house this morning, and Joe was trying to catch it. Tina must have seen him from the window, and she followed them. He didn't even realize it until they got to the cemetery," Chris said.

The tears kept flooding down Robin's face.

"Why didn't he bring her back sooner?" Jeff asked.

"When she saw the cemetery, she stopped because she had a picture or something in her pocket for her Poppy. So she asked Joe to help her find a grave, and before he could bring her home, the puppy took off again. Tina ran after him. She was just an excited kid playing with a puppy. Joe kept chasing her, wanting them both to be safe."

"Ma'am," someone said from behind Chris. "I'm so sorry. I wouldn't harm that little angel, no way," Robin looked up to see a shabbily dressed man who wasn't much older than forty. She could tell his apology was sincere. His eyes looked at Tina tenderly.

Tina had always been quick to capture the hearts of those she associated with.

"Oh no, I forgot to call Mom," Robin said.

"No worries," Jeff said. "I gave her a call. Chris helped with the number. She'll call the others. We really should get her home though. The snow is still coming down."

Tina stood looking at Jeff and then back at her mom. A smile shone across her face as she took Jeff's hand and then her mom's.

They walked to the car in silence, each feeling a strong connection.

To anyone observing them, they looked like a typical family heading out in the snow. Chris knew God was up to something.

"Pastor, maybe we should pray for them," Joe said, watching them too.

"What would you like to pray about, Joe?"

"Let's pray that our little angel gets her mom and dad back together. That's all she could talk about, and of course, she wants Blackie."

Despite the fact that lunch was ready, everyone was eager to pray and give praise to God for keeping Tina safe. They also prayed for healing for the family.

Pete invited Chris to stay for lunch. After getting a warm drink and some soup, he headed to a table by the window where Joe sat.

"Joe, you still look for strays?"

"Yes, sir, that's my job. Poor babies. People don't take care for their babies."

"I was amazed at how many cats and dogs you keep in the alley behind the factory. Do the people in the factory know you're back there?"

"Sure do. They don't use that fenced area, and most don't want those animals starving. The factory workers stop by with their scraps."

"Interesting. Now Joe, could you tell me more about what Tina talked to you about?"

"Mostly she played tag with the puppy. She chased him, and he jumped all over her. She sure took a liking to him. But he liked her just as much."

"Did she say anything about her family?"

"She said her dad finally came home. That little one has been praying for him with her poppy for a long time. She wants her mom to let him live with them."

Chris was astonished at how much Tina understood. Why would Nate do that?

"Well, thanks for letting me join you for lunch. I've got to get home while I can. You keep those babies safe and warm."

Joe smiled and turned back to look out the window—always on the lookout for strays.

Chris stood near the counter and looked around the shelter. Broken people, but caring, faith-filled people down on their luck. People down in the valley of their life but truly putting their hope in God. Their prayers were heartfelt, and they had put someone else's need ahead of their own. They were people waiting and believing God to find relief from their troubles.

Chris thought about a book he read when he was in the seminary—*In His Steps* by Charles M. Sheldon. It was about Christian people genuinely living like Jesus did. Written over a hundred years ago, it was meant to change the people in big churches who live well and ignore the people who live close who are in need. Some of the congregation took a challenge to live like Jesus did.

The events of the day had stirred his heart and thoughts. Things were going to change for a lot of people, including himself.

CHAPTER 28

Pulling into Betty's driveway was difficult. Someone had done some snow blowing in the driveway, but the snowplow had left a huge pile of snow at the end of the driveway. Over nine inches of snow covered his car. It would take him hours to shovel out, and steady snowfall made the task impossible. Whoever did the driveway cleared a pathway around his car, blowing the snow toward his car.

Betty came running out the back door. Tina got out of the car and raced to her. Robin looked on and smiled.

"A few weeks ago, I would have never thought that was possible. Now, I don't think I can imagine anything more natural. What a miracle!" she said to Jeff.

"Robin, what now? Do you want me to leave you all to talk? What are you thinking?" he asked.

Moments passed before she answered.

Finally she said, "Jeff, the roads are bad, and I wouldn't want you out there. Take a good look at your car. I'm sure Mom is ready for a late lunch by now, so why don't you join us? Unless you needed to leave."

"Really? Are you sure?"

"One step at a time, Jeff. I can't promise you anything. I'm tired. Do you think you could help me to the house? It looks slippery."

"Stay put, and I'll come around to your side." Jeff slid a little as he walked around the car. He had not prepared for this wintry weather.

Jeff helped her up the back steps, and when they came through the kitchen door, Tina and Betty were already busy getting food ready. They whispered and laughed without immediately noticing them. Four places were set at the table again. Tina's card was between J and Mom. He *was* J.

Betty said, "Jeff, this is our Christmas smorgasbord. So many people dropped off food that we have enough for a week. It will be a few more minutes, so why don't you and Robin go in the family room?"

Observing Jeff's thin socks, Betty said, "Tina, why don't you go find Poppy's slippers and bring them here?"

Tina knew they were in the front entranceway, and she brought them right back. Jeff put them on, and they fit perfectly.

Robin and Jeff talked for a few minutes about what had transpired with Tina, Joe, and the puppy. They agreed about the need to talk to Tina later about her actions and then include a conversation about Jeff.

Betty called from the kitchen, and they went in. "Let's join hands and for a blessing," Betty said.

"Lord, thank you for bringing our Tina home safely. Bless this food and this family. Thank you for our visitor and this fellowship time. We give praise and thanksgiving for being such a *big God*. And all God's people said. *Amen*," they all chimed in.

Tina talked nonstop about the puppy and Joe. The puppy excited her. In Rochester their apartment did not allow pets, so the subject never came up.

Robin didn't have the heart to scold her too much, but they would talk to her about wandering off. Funny, as a child she chased after every puppy she found too.

"Robin, do you remember the shabby little border collie you brought home that time? What did you call her?"

"Bandit. I do remember how much I loved that dog. I couldn't believe you let me keep her."

"You had your father wrapped around your finger, and you persuaded him."

"Oh, I don't know. As I recall, I wasn't the only one attached to that dog," Robin said and laughed.

Tina jumped up from the table, and they heard her going upstairs. When she came back, she held a picture of Robin with a dog.

"Momma, is that Bandit?" she asked.

That picture had been one of Robin's favorite pictures.

"Mom, how old was I in this picture?" she asked.

"Look at the back. I date all my pictures," Betty replied.

She took the picture out of the frame and realized she was the same age as Tina. At that moment, they all realized why Tina had been so fascinated by the puppy.

"I can't believe how much she is like you, Robin," Betty said.

"Scary, isn't it?"

"Why you were always my precious little one. Normal behavior for all kids."

Looks like we're getting a puppy, Robin thought. Jeff just listened to the conversation as he ate. The food was amazing. He was learning a lot about Robin's childhood. It seemed like all children loved puppies.

When they finished lunch, Betty, Tina, and Jeff cleared the dishes. Robin was pretty exhausted, more from stress than anything else.

"Robin, let me help you upstairs," Betty said.

"But Jeff …"

"Jeff and Tina will be here when you come back. By the looks of the snow, he'll be here for a while."

There was almost a foot of snow, and it was still coming down, although not as heavy.

Tina and Jeff went into the family room behind Betty and Robin.

The room had not changed much since his last visit, although he never envisioned being here with his daughter someday.

Tina had drawing materials out on a nearby table and was ready to make a picture.

"She's quite the artist too. Wait until you see what she can do," Betty said as she came back into the room.

"I think I saw a drawing she made at the Christmas Eve service," he answered.

"You were there?" Betty said.

He nodded his head.

Tina looked up at him and gave him a smile.

"Before you say anything—"

Betty stopped him. "Jeff, I'm glad you came to the program, and I think Tina is too. Aren't you?"

Tina nodded as she listened.

"Jeff, love is unconditional like Jesus taught us. And like Tina has taught us, right, honey?"

"Yes, Jesus loves us," Tina responded.

"Jeff, can you take a look at something in the kitchen for me?" she asked. "Tina, we will be right back. Let me put the TV on for you. Momma is sleeping. Promise me you will stay right here," Betty said.

"I will," Tina said.

Out in the kitchen, Betty continued, "Jeff, I didn't want to talk in front of her. I hurt Tina and Nate too. I hurt Robin the most, and she was my only daughter. God is a God of second chances. I've been given one. You will get yours if you ask."

"How can you say that? What I did …"

"Jeff, it's clear you love both of them. I sense how you feel, and I'm sure they do. Look at Tina." They both peeked in the family room. "Everyone she meets loves her. She melts their hearts with her loving personality."

"I felt such a connection from the first moment I met her at Chris's house. I just jumped to ignorant conclusions based on mere speculation. If only I had done some research or talked to people."

"Jeff, don't dwell on the past. You can't change it, but you can change your future with God's help."

"How?"

"Ask God's forgiveness, and then forgive yourself. Robin and Tina already have. I do too."

Betty could see the tears well up in his eyes.

"I'll be right back. I need some fresh air," he said.

He grabbed his coat, which hung on a kitchen hook, and went out to look at the snow. The deep snow prevented him from getting on his knees, but he just looked up toward heaven and poured out his heart.

He wanted forgiveness, a second chance with Tina, and a second chance as a husband.

The snow was slowing down, and the sun began to set. It was later than he thought.

"Jeff, come on in. Tina has something she wants to show you," Betty called from the porch door.

With a deep desire for an opportunity at a new life with Tina included and possibly Robin, he entered the house filled with hope.

Chris got home later than he planned. The day after Christmas was supposed to be his quiet day, but not today. Despite the inconvenience, he praised God for a happy ending.

Kristen came to the door to greet him.

"You've had an eventful day, haven't you?" she asked, knowing most of what happened with Tina.

"That's an understatement. I am so relieved they found Tina before the snow piled up any higher. It's beautiful out there but not for a lost little girl."

"From what you told me on the phone, it seems like Robin and Jeff put their differences aside and focused on Tina," Kristen said.

"Actually, if I wasn't acquainted with their history, I'd think they were still married. Jeff showed concern for both Tina and Robin."

"Do you think Jeff still loves Robin?" she asked.

"I don't think he ever stopped. He's just a guy who was taken in by worldly things and desires. He honestly didn't understand what he would give up. People are so misinformed about abortions," he said.

"Maybe Jeff can help with his testimony," Kristen said.

"This family's story has profoundly impacted this community. Many people helped look for Tina. The patrons at the homeless center today put aside their own needs, and I learned so much by being there. The

Lord is flooding my heart with ideas. Our church can expand mission outreach in many ways," he said.

Kristen hugged him. "Even our children think differently now, and I think children should be included in those opportunities. Two tragedies, yet God got us through it. The congregation will never be the same."

"Look at our children. Think about Tina. Children fill our lives more than money ever could, and we are fortunate to have them. Didn't Jesus say we are to be childlike?"

Chris watched his children in the family room getting ready to play a game on the family room floor. Such a simple game, but he knew in a minute they would be having a ball.

"Some people keep searching for happiness to fill a void that can only be filled with Jesus and his love. Once they find his unconditional love and enter into relationship with him, the void will be filled," Chris said.

"Well, I am hoping Jeff and Robin will find love again. I talked to him at the coffee shop this morning, and he is filled with regrets for past mistakes."

"While you spent time with Jeff at the coffee shop, I was with Betty. She is healing but revealed Nate told Tina about Jeff some time ago," Chris said.

"She amazes me. How did she keep that secret? I don't think she was looking for Jeff today though. I think she was just chasing that puppy." They both laughed. All kids love puppies, and their children were begging for one too.

"Looking back, raising Tina by herself helped Robin grow into the strong Christian she is today. Understanding why she suffered like she did is impossible, but God's plans brought them all to this moment. As you know, dark periods often lead to tremendous blessings," Chris said.

"For Tina's sake, I hope she gets her dream of a family with Jeff in it."

CHAPTER 29

Jeff and Tina spent over an hour just talking as she colored, and they watched a holiday special on TV. Betty settled back in her chair, watching their interactions, noting Tina's beaming face each time she looked at Jeff.

Soon Robin came down the stairs. The color was back in her cheeks, and she looked content with what she saw.

They all decided to raid the refrigerator for snacks. Tina insisted everyone eat more of the birthday cake and put the candles back on so she could make another wish.

She asked if they wanted to play the Operation game she got for Christmas. The four of them played and laughed until Robin reminded Tina of her eight o'clock bedtime.

"Tina, it is time for bed now. Run up and Momma will be up in a minute."

Tina hesitated for a moment and looked at Jeff before she finally left the room.

"Robin, it's late. Jeff isn't going to have time to dig out. Do you mind if he sleeps in the office upstairs on that pullout sofa?"

Robin hesitated to answer because she didn't want to give him false hope. But he really had helped this morning, and Tina enjoyed his presence.

"No, Mom, I don't mind. Thanks for asking. I'm going to get her into bed now."

Jeff felt relief that Robin had said yes. He would still need to go to the car for his bags. When he returned, Robin hadn't reappeared.

Betty was unwinding in front of the television, and he joined her. After a couple of hours, she said, "Jeff, I'm going to call it a night. Let me show you where you are staying. The office has a TV and a phone. Use the bathroom next to the office. Make yourself comfortable."

Jeff picked up his bags and followed Betty upstairs. They knew that Robin and Tina were in their rooms, so he walked down the hallway quietly.

"Have a good night, Jeff. See you in the morning, and sleep in as long as you want to," Betty said.

"Thanks. I think I can find everything okay."

She turned and went down the hall.

Waking up in Betty's house seemed like a dream to Jeff. A few days ago he presumed chances of being part of Tina's life were impossible. As he finished dressing, he smelled coffee and heard voices downstairs. He wondered what the day would bring.

"Good morning, Jeff. Help yourself to some coffee and the goodies on the counter," Betty said as he entered the kitchen.

Robin and Tina were already eating at the table. Tina looked up, and he noticed the empty chair next to her.

Jeff picked up some coffee cake and what looked like a breakfast casserole. He also took some of the fruit. He set the plate down next to Tina and went back to grab a cup of coffee.

"Sorry I disappeared last night. Guess my energy level still isn't normal yet," Robin said.

"Robin, remember the doctors said full recovery takes time. Maybe you need to take a little more time off from work. I told Susan you would give her a call," Betty said. She looked at Robin with motherly concern.

"Betty is right, Robin. You were wiped out yesterday. There was stress added to the usual holiday stress. You need a day to rest. Maybe

I can help out with Tina for a few days, and you can rest up?" he said sincerely.

"What about your job?" Robin asked.

"I have a lot of vacation time accumulated, and Christmas is the slow time anyway. I've already told my secretary I'm out for three weeks."

"Three weeks? Here?" Robin asked.

Jeff looked into her eyes. "Robin, I'm taking things one day at a time. I promise, I'm not here to cause problems for you. I want to help. Let me. I think you and Betty have had a very stressful time lately. Am I right?" he asked.

Before Robin could answer, she noted Tina standing behind Jeff waiting for her response.

"We do need help. These past few weeks have been challenging. Tina and I haven't even unpacked everything stored in the garage."

"That would be a big help, Jeff," Betty added. "But how about we take a few days to just relax? This is still the holiday season."

"Today is your day with your mom to relax. I'll take Tina out. Okay?" he asked.

"Yes."

"Yeah!" Tina exclaimed. "Can Blackie come home too?"

"Blackie, I forgot. Joe still has Blackie," Robin said.

"Are we getting a dog?" Betty asked.

Robin, Tina, and Jeff all looked at her face and laughed as they all said, "*Please!*"

Betty laughed too. "Wasn't so long ago I was all alone. A family can't be complete without a puppy. Thank you, Lord!"

"I guess that's a yes, Tina," Jeff said. "We need to get some puppy supplies though."

"Jeff, how about you take Tina to the center to see if you can make arrangements?" Robin asked.

"Tina, I need to go out and try to find my car under all the snow. Then do you want to come with me so Momma can rest?"

She smiled and shook her head yes.

"Jeff, I would feel better if you take my car. It is better in the snow, and there will be less shoveling," Robin said.

"That would be great. Tina, I will be ready in about ten minutes."

Betty said, "I'll help you put your snow clothes on. It is still pretty cold out there, and don't forget, there is so much snow."

Betty and Tina left the two of them alone in the kitchen.

"Robin, tell me what's going on in your mind," Jeff said.

"This all seems so … natural. I don't want Tina to get her hopes up and think this will be more than it is."

"Robin, this is real. I won't hurt her, and I will *never* hurt you again. Believe me when I say that."

"Jeff, I want to believe you. Though I have forgiven you, the pain you caused went deep. This is hard. I'm not sure I can trust you again," she said. His eyes told her he meant it, but she remembered the broken vows he didn't keep.

"All ready," Tina said, coming into the room. She was dressed in snow pants and a jacket.

"Wow, I didn't even start shoveling," Jeff said.

"Go ahead, Jeff. Here are Nate's snow boots. I'll help Tina with her boots, and I'll send her out in a minute," said Betty.

Jeff went out the back door and started the car to warm it up. Betty handed him a shovel, and a few minutes later, Tina came out.

She had never shoveled snow before, but she had fun copying him. Robin and Betty watched from the window. The snow was light enough for her to carry off to the side. Then she got distracted and laid in the snow to make snow angels. She called and motioned to him to do it too. Despite the fact he lacked proper snow clothing, he joined her. His business coat was long enough to cover his pants. Robin's heart melted when she saw how happy Tina appeared. She took a picture with her cell phone, wondering if this was a onetime thing.

Robin sat down at the table after she poured another cup of coffee.

"Mom, am I making a mistake?"

"Honey, I think only you can answer that. What are you feeling in your heart? Open it up like you did for me. Chris said we should ask for

God's will and wisdom in our choices. You made the right choice with Tina, and I am confident you will again."

"You're right. God helped me then, and I keep hearing a small voice say, 'Trust me.' My heart tells me to let Jeff in—that this is real, the way it was meant to be. I think of the Bible story about Hosea. He loved his wife after everything she had done. What a great love story."

"Robin, I think you said the word *love*. Guess God already gave you your answer." Betty took Robin's hand and squeezed it.

Robin continued watching Tina and Jeff until they pulled out of the driveway.

Robin's thoughts confused her. Was she falling in love again? Would she let him back in, or would he take Tina?

CHAPTER 30

Joe was at the center having coffee when Jeff and Tina arrived. His face lit up when he saw them together again.

"Joe, has anyone claimed Blackie yet?" Jeff asked.

"No, not yet. There weren't any tags, and by the looks of her, she was abandoned," Joe said. "Why do you ask?"

"Tina wants to keep him. Her mom said it's okay. What do you think? Can this little one care for a puppy?" Jeff asked.

"He couldn't find a better owner," Joe said.

"Grandma's house doesn't have what a puppy needs. Does it, Tina?"

"No," was all she said. She kept looking anxiously at Joe.

"Don't worry, Tina. You'll have Blackie soon."

Jeff made arrangements with Joe to pick the puppy up in a few hours. Joe helped Tina make a list of all they would need. Finding a good home for a stray gave him immense satisfaction.

Jeff and Tina left the center and headed to Bailey's Pet Store, which was a short walk away. Bailey's Pet Store hadn't changed since Jeff was a boy. His grandparents had lived close by, and he had spent his summers in Lima. Tina immediately went over to the pets when they entered. Jeff was not letting her out of his sight after yesterday's scare. He headed over to the caged animals and found Tina chatting with an employee.

"She sure loves animals," came a voice behind him.

"Yes, she ... are you Shannon Bailey?" he asked.

"I am, and you are?"

"Jeff Anderson. I used to be best friends with your brother Mark in college, and when I visited my grandparents. I came to your house. You were the painful little sister who always pestered us."

"Oh, really? Well now I help run the family store. What can I help you with?" she asked.

"My daughter is getting a puppy, and we need some supplies," he said, pointing to Tina.

"Isn't that Tina?" Shannon asked.

"Do you know her?" Jeff asked.

"Sure, she sang at the Christmas Eve service. What a sweet voice. Seems like everyone is still talking about it. We all got calls to pray yesterday. Glad everything turned out okay," she said, smiling. "Tina, let me see your list."

Shannon looked the list over. "You are in luck. We happen to have everything on the list. Time to bring out your wallet, Anderson. Nothing but the best for this little angel." Tina smiled, and Shannon took her hand.

By the time they finished, they had everything on the list, including a bed and puppy toys. Jeff wanted to spoil her and buy extra things, but he suddenly found himself remembering to be a parent. Robin might be upset if he went overboard.

Watching Jeff and Tina interact amused Shannon. He read every label and compared prices. He was very different from his college days. *Does Mark know he's in town?*

As Jeff and Tina were finishing collecting their items for checkout, Shannon sent a text message to her brother Mark: *Mark, Jeff Anderson is here at the store. You will never guess who his daughter is. It's the little cutie that sang at church on Christmas Eve. Text me if you can come to the store.*

As Shannon was checking them out, her phone buzzed.

"Excuse me for just a sec," she said. "Jeff, Mark just texted me. He'll be here in five minutes and asked if you could meet him at the Bookstore Cafe. He said he had something urgent to talk to you about. Can you meet him there?" she asked.

"Mark? Tell him I would love to see him. What could so important?" he said.

"He didn't say," she answered. Shannon sent another message and finished checking them out.

"Tina, are you up for some hot chocolate?" he asked.

"Cookie too?" she asked.

"Cookie too," he said, laughing.

"Can I look at the fish one more time?" she asked.

"Sure, go ahead. There's time," he said. Jeff was a little more comfortable now that he knew the layout of the store, but he kept her in his sight. The old-fashioned cowbell on the door jingled when someone came in anyway.

"Say, Jeff. Do you mind if I ask you a question?"

"No. I don't mind. You're like my little sister. What's up?" he answered.

"Are you and Robin still an item?" she asked.

She caught him off guard. How could he answer without explaining how despicable he had been about Tina?

Finally he responded, "Tina is our child, and we both love her, so I guess we are an item of sorts. We are divorced." He stopped talking because Tina was already coming back.

Shannon helped them get all the packages together. The bags of puppy chow meant separate trips for him.

"I'll watch her while you take this stuff out. The snow from the plow makes it difficult to walk around," Shannon said.

When he came back, Shannon said, "Come back real soon."

She watched Jeff and Tina walk hand in hand to the cafe. Jeff looked so attached to Tina, but his facial expressions when he tried to explain his relationship with Robin showed pain. Mark's text alarmed her. His message sounded like a legal thing.

Father, please help him find his way. Heal that family, she prayed.

With the roads being cleared, the cafe was bustling. Yesterday he sat here with Kristen talking about the daughter who now held his hand. His life had changed in a day. How was that possible so quickly? Answered prayers? His newfound belief in them made him realize his prayers had been answered.

Jeff let Tina place her own order and then ordered a gingerbread latte for himself. A familiar voice was calling to him.

"Jeff, over here." He turned toward the voice and saw Mark sitting with a woman at a table away from the counter. He recognized him instantly.

"Mark, it's great to see you, buddy. Been what—about ten years?" Jeff asked. "Too long. We were going to keep in touch. Remember?"

"Life will do that," Mark answered. "Aren't you going to introduce us?"

"Mark, this is my daughter, Tina," Jeff said.

"Hi, Tina. You did a great job singing on Christmas Eve," he said.

Tina smiled and said, "Thank you." She acted a little embarrassed.

Tina put her hot chocolate down and gave Mark an unexpected hug. He hugged her back without hesitation.

"I was so excited when Shannon sent me a text. So much has changed for me and I guess for you too," he said, smiling at Tina.

"Tina, Jeff, this is my wife, Cathy."

Tina gave her a hug too, and they sat back down.

"Tina, where did you learn how to sing? Not from your dad?" he asked.

Jeff answered, "I don't sing. Must be from Robin."

"How is Robin? We couldn't talk to her at the church. The service was crowded, and the kids kept us busy."

Mark gave Cathy a look. Then Cathy said, "Tina, I wondered if you would like to take your hot chocolate and go in the back to listen to a special story in a few minutes? Jeff?"

"Honey, would you like to hear the story?" Jeff asked.

"Sure," she answered.

"We'll be back in about thirty minutes, Jeff. Our kids are back there with their aunt." Cathy helped Tina with her hot chocolate and cookie.

Mark and Jeff took a few minutes to catch up on family news and jobs. Both acknowledged how fast ten years passed.

"Learned Associates offered me a job about the same time you moved. Remember, you came in to file—"

"You can say it man. Divorce. I was so stupid and unreasonable back then," Jeff said.

"Stupid about what exactly?" Mark probed.

"I came to file for divorce because Robin wouldn't have an abortion. All I could think about was my own career. Luckily, she didn't listen to me," Jeff said.

"Help me understand. The career didn't work out?" Mark asked.

"Mark, I am at the top in my career, but life there is lonely and not fulfilling. Something was always missing. No relationship ever amounted to anything. My life's pretty empty. What I want now is what I had ten years ago."

"When you came to me to file for divorce, you were so angry. I couldn't talk you. Then you up and left town so fast. You never contacted me again," Mark said.

"Mark, I'm sorry for that too. I didn't listen to anybody. My parents told me to take some time to think. I was angry. She was my soul mate," he said.

His statement surprised Mark. When he came to Mark's office ten years ago, he was adamant that he wanted a divorce. He couldn't leave Robin fast enough, and there was no talk of other options.

"So you and Robin—anything going on now?" Mark asked.

"Mark, these past few days opened my eyes to possibilities. Robin and I never stayed in touch after I left here. I am ashamed to say, I didn't even know about Tina until recently."

"Do you mean you didn't pay child support or alimony?" he asked.

Jeff looked at him blankly. "No, I didn't. She never asked me for anything."

"I honestly don't remember the details of your agreement I drew up, but I'm sure I included some type of alimony at least. I moved the same year you did. Something is not right here. Did you look at papers?" Mark asked Jeff.

"I didn't give a new address. I lived in a hotel until I got settled in my new job," Jeff said.

"Let me do some checking. I'm in town until after New Year's Day. Where can I reach you?" Mark asked.

"Here's my cell number on my card," he said, handing him a business card. "I'm staying with Robin and her mother, Betty."

"You two in the same house?" Mark asked.

"That's right, in the same house. You remember her mom, Betty Johnson—big house in town," Jeff said.

"I remember. So are you two back together?" he asked.

Jeff looked at him. "I wish. I love Tina and Robin, but I've made *huge* mistakes. I was lucky I got Robin the first time."

Cathy came up to the table with Tina. "You guys catch up?" she asked. "We had a great time." She hugged Tina. "What a sweetheart. These are our children, Tim and Megan."

Jeff smiled at them. They were younger than Tina, but with Tina's developmental delays, they got along fine.

"Hi. Thanks for letting her share time with your kids. We would like Tina to play with the kids again before we leave. Would you guys like that?"

They both said yes. "We need to get our pet supplies home so we'll be ready to pick up Tina's puppy."

"Puppy?" asked Tim.

"*Oops*—wrong word, Jeff," Mark said. "Kids and puppies—you will have them at your house until we leave." Everyone laughed, and Tina squealed with excitement.

Mark and Cathy sat back down as Jeff and Tina walked away. They came to the same conclusion Shannon had. Tina and Jeff loved being together.

"You know, Cathy, ten years ago, I couldn't picture Jeff being the caring father of a little girl. His anger was out of control after the genetic testing. He couldn't run fast enough. Now he wishes he could turn back the clock."

"I can imagine how crushed he is now. She might not be what he expected as a young parent, but she is beautiful despite her disabilities. I wonder how many people are quick to make the same mistake," Cathy said.

"Probably more than I care to guess. Jeff's a good guy who made a selfish choice. We all do. I wish you knew him like I did growing up. When Shannon sent me the text, I felt this urgency about meeting up with Jeff. I am concerned about his divorce papers. I realized I never finished working on them because I switched firms. Something doesn't seem right. I need to check in and see what happened with the papers while I am in town. Do you mind if I stop by my old firm tomorrow?" he asked.

"You do what you want tomorrow. We might go sledding. Right, kids?" Cathy asked.

"Maybe the puppy wants to go sledding," Megan said.

Mark laughed. "Like I told Jeff—kids and puppies."

"Mr. Bailey, we need to return your children to their grandmother. She loves her time with the grandkids and planned the whole night with the kids so you and I can go to Luigi's," Cathy said.

"Sounds like a plan," he said and took her hand. The kids were ahead of them talking about Tina's puppy.

CHAPTER 31

Tina could not stop talking about her puppy. The whole experience of shopping and planning seemed so natural. In his head he envisioned training the puppy as a family. He was proud of his daughter and wasn't afraid for people to see it.

Suddenly, his thoughts went to his parents. *Wonder what Mom and Dad would think about Tina and Robin?* Sometime in the near future he would need to tell them the truth.

Betty and Robin were in the kitchen when they pulled into the driveway. Tina helped him carry the bags in.

"There you are. I started to worry about you being lost. You've been gone a while," Robin said, greeting them at the door.

Jeff detected an anxious look on her face. "Robin, you can trust me. Really. Let Tina share what we bought while I bring the rest in."

"Okay," she responded.

Tina giggled. "Look, Momma." She stood proudly holding up a cute little puppy collar. Robin loved seeing her so happy.

After three trips, Jeff came in and announced, "Last of it."

"How about you … Dad? Are you worn out yet?"

"This afternoon was enjoyable, and I'm not tired at all. She is so excited about the puppy. Do you think we should go over some rules or anything before we pick the puppy up?" he asked.

"Maybe we all, including Mom, should talk about it after dinner. You're staying for dinner and overnight, aren't you?" Robin asked.

"Would I be imposing or overextending my stay?" he asked.

Robin waited a moment to answer. "No, not at all. I would say staying was just for Tina's benefit, but that wouldn't be the truth."

Jeff looked into her eyes, and he saw the way she looked back at him had changed from yesterday. Years ago she had looked at him the same way. He began to hope. *Lord, please help us find our way back to love.*

"What is the truth about me staying?" he asked.

"I want Tina to know her father, and I would like to feel comfortable with you being around her," she said.

They both realized Tina and Betty were looking on and waiting for something.

"Can Tina help with dinner later? We need to go to pick up the puppy at the center. I talked to Joe, and he is going to meet us shortly. Did you want to come?" he asked.

"No, I'll let you guys handle the puppy. Dinner will be more leftovers from Christmas. And Jeff, we do need to talk. Okay?" she asked.

"Okay, but I'm warning you—puppies are busy," he responded.

"Don't forget that this grandma knows how to handle puppies. Did you two want to go out to Luigi's for dinner tonight so you can talk?" Betty asked.

"Robin?"

"Wow, dinner out. I haven't been to Luigi's in forever. Tina, okay if Momma goes out tonight?" Robin asked.

"Momma, Grandma and I will watch Blackie," she said.

Robin's fluttery stomach confused her, but she finally said, "It's a …"

"Date," Jeff said and winked at Tina.

"That's settled. You two have fun picking up the puppy, and Robin, why don't you relax in the tub?"

"Grandma's giving out orders. We better behave and follow them," Robin said, laughing.

The room emptied, and all Betty could do was smile.

Late afternoon at the center was a little busy. People came in early to get warm before dinner.

Jeff was still amazed how they all greeted Tina. She kept searching for Joe, and Jeff noticed how controlled she was. Robin had done a great job raising her.

The door finally opened and Joe entered with Blackie in his arms.

"Hey little angel, here he is," he said handing the puppy to her.

"I checked at the Humane Society, and no one has reported a lost dog. You still need to take him for shots, license, etc.," he said.

"Thanks for the reminder. And thanks for all you do with those animals. That's such a good thing. You've made this little one so happy," Jeff said.

"She is a delight," he said, watching her with the puppy. "Now no more chasing other puppies. Joe cares for them."

"Okay," said Tina.

Jeff and Tina said their goodbyes and started home. Blackie sat on Tina's lap and licked her face constantly. Good thing it was a short ride home.

Betty greeted them at the door this time. "Dinner is almost ready, Tina. Maybe Dad can watch the puppy while you wash up and eat."

Jeff took the puppy and continued to play with it.

"Robin is getting ready. She will be down in a minute." Things seemed so natural now. "Jeff, please don't hurt my daughter by leading her on. She's had too much pain in her life already."

"Betty, you don't have to worry about me," he said.

Tina came in and sat at the table to eat. She said her blessing and ate quietly so she could play with the puppy.

Robin walked into the kitchen dressed in a black dress and looked amazing.

"Robin, you look more rested tonight. Must be a day to rest helped," he said.

"It did. I certainly feel more rested. Maybe after New Year's I'll go back to work. Susan called and said she had something to talk to me about. I hope I am not losing my job," she said.

"Susan raves about you," Betty said. "You won't lose your job. She just wants to make sure you're up to coming back."

"You're probably right," Robin replied.

Jeff sensed job security worried Robin. He would need to talk to her about helping out with expenses. He owed her a lot.

"Ready for a great Italian dinner, Mr. Anderson?" Robin asked.

"Give me a minute to change, and we'll be off," he said.

He had a few clothes in his suitcase that he wanted to wear tonight too. A few minutes later, he walked into the kitchen.

"Who is taking care of this puppy tonight?" he asked.

"Me," was Tina's response.

"Okay, Grandma and Momma, what do we want to do about the rules?" he said.

"Rules?" Tina asked.

"Yes, honey. We need you to clean up after puppy and feed her every day," Robin said. "She needs to stay in the crate sometimes."

Tina looked surprised.

"Maybe we could do this tomorrow. This is puppy's first night, and we don't want puppy scared, do we?" Robin said, looking at Jeff and Betty. They both agreed.

"Momma is going out now. Be good and listen to Grandma," she said.

Robin knew Tina wouldn't let the puppy out of her sight.

"Ready?" Jeff asked. He helped her with her coat and felt breathless when they touched. Feelings buried years ago surprised him.

What did the Bible say about putting on a new self and living a new life, forgetting the past? *Lord, I'm believing!*

CHAPTER 32

Robin and Jeff both sensed a little awkwardness walking into the restaurant. They hadn't gone out for dinner since way back before the pregnancy testing. Issues between them were not resolved, but they needed to talk about Tina. Neither knew what to expect.

Italian food had always been their favorite. During their lean days, they would have pizza on Christmas Eve because they couldn't afford to travel to Lima to visit family. But on date night, when things were good, they would go out for Italian food.

Betty had made reservations, and the waitress seated them quickly.

"Wow, it's been quite some time since I've had real Italian food. This is a nice place. Thanks for taking me out, Jeff," Robin said.

"I'm happy you agreed to come. With our rocky past, I understand this can't be comfortable, but you've dealt with so much recently I figured you deserved a special night out. How do you feel about leaving your mom with Tina and the puppy?" he asked.

"Mom has significantly changed these past few weeks. She hardened her heart ten years ago when I made my decision and cut me out of her life. I understood the initial shock, but she never got over it, and Dad couldn't even get her to budge. The accident changed her, and once she opened her heart to love—well, she's the mom I used to know," she said.

"Both of us were ignorant and unreliable, and pride prevented us from admitting our mistakes. We jumped to the wrong conclusion about Down syndrome," Jeff said.

"You both abandoned me at a difficult time. I joined a support group, and they helped me before and after Tina was born. My dad was a great support. Not long ago Mom asked for my forgiveness, and we are leaving the past behind. I admit my pride created problems too," she said.

"Excuse me, are you ready to order, or do you need more time?" the waitress asked.

"Wine, Robin?" he asked.

"A glass of pinot grigio please," she said.

"I'll have the same, and when you come back, we'll ready to order," Jeff said.

Robin found Jeff's handling of the waitress attractive and reminiscent of the Friday nights in Rochester.

"Let me guess what you will order," he said.

"Maybe I changed my taste," Robin said.

"No, you're having chicken marsala. That's my guess," he said.

Robin laughed. "You got me, and I bet you're having lasagna."

"You're right on that. Maybe we haven't changed that much."

The dinner was great. Jeff filled Robin in on the pet store, homeless shelter, and then meeting Mark. He never brought up the divorce papers because he wanted the evening to just be pleasant.

"So tell me about your job," he said.

Robin explained how she had lost her job in Rochester due to downsizing and how her current job was temporary until something else opened up.

Jeff ordered one tiramisu to share—their favorite desert. As they ate, Jeff looked adoringly in her eyes. Both felt a strong connection and reawakening of the desire to touch, and Robin's cheeks turned rosy.

"Do you think we should call Mom to see how the puppy thing is going?" Robin asked, breaking the silence.

"She would call if she needs us. I don't want this evening to end," Jeff said.

Robin smiled. She didn't either. She had never dated because she refused to leave Tina with anyone except Marcy or her dad, though other friends had offered. The wall around her heart protected her and her child from pain caused by relationships.

"Hey, you two. How are you?"

Robin and Jeff looked up. Mark stood next to the table with his wife, Cathy. Mark introduced Cathy to Robin.

"Mind if we join you for coffee?" Mark asked.

"Second cup with you today. You'll be up all night," Jeff said.

"Don't worry. When we're home, we Baileys are up to all hours. Right, Cathy?" Mark said.

"They sure are—hard core, competitive foosball players. They don't stop until way past midnight," Cathy said.

They sat for a little while exchanging stories about the kids. It was nice to see him again after all these years.

"We could talk all night, but with a new puppy we should rescue Mom," Robin said.

"Our kids are insisting on seeing Tina and the puppy. Jeff has my number. We'll be here through New Year's. Give us a call, or the kids will call," Mark said.

"I will," Jeff said, relieved he didn't bring up the divorce papers.

Mark turned to Cathy on the way out. "Remind me to check on those papers. I could be wrong, but I think those two are getting back together."

"I hope so. With faith all things are possible," Cathy said.

Tina played with the puppy in the family room as Betty watched TV. It didn't take long for Betty to make rules like no chasing indoors and no puppy food in the family room. The rest would have to wait until Robin and Jeff got back. Betty hoped they were having a great time at dinner. She was getting used to having Jeff around. When Nate died, the house had been so empty. Now it felt wonderful to have this family and her church family back.

"Tina, time for bed, sweetie," Betty said.

"What about puppy?" Tina asked.

"Daddy bought that crate for puppy. Remember, puppies do things and chew things, so he has to stay in the crate," Betty said.

Tina had a sad look, which bothered Betty, but she wasn't certain what to do. She put the puppy in the crate in the kitchen, and Tina went up to get ready for bed.

Betty went up to help her. When Tina finished in the bathroom, Betty went in to tuck her in. They could hear Blackie in the kitchen whining. Tina didn't say anything but looked at Betty.

"All right, the crate can come up to your room. But puppy stays in the crate unless someone like Momma, Dad, or I take her out. Do you understand?" she said.

Tina shook her head. "I promise!"

She jumped up and went downstairs. Blackie was glad to see her. Betty carried the crate up to the bedroom. She turned the lights off and stood in the hallway listening.

Tina talked softly to Blackie. "You have to be quiet. Shh! It'll be okay." She hummed the song "Jesus Loves Me."

Betty laughed to herself. *Always thinking of you, Lord. And oh, she does love you. Thank you for giving me this opportunity to love this child. Thank you for your forgiveness and blessings you have given me.*

CHAPTER 33

Robin and Jeff relaxed on the way home. The evening was enjoyable.

"Jeff, thank you for dinner. It brought back memories for me. Good ones," Robin said.

"I'm glad. We did have some good times," Jeff said. "I spent time with Mark at the coffee shop this afternoon. When we were younger, we never envisioned ourselves with kids. He looks like he is a natural."

"Jeff, I've watched you these couple of days. You are picking up this father thing yourself," she said.

"Words can't say how sorry I am for letting you down in the past. Let me be there for Tina and you from now on," Jeff said.

Robin didn't answer. Instead she said, "I didn't know Mark moved. When did he move?"

"Surprisingly, just after I left, a big firm made him got a good job offer, and he moved. Mark met Cathy after moving."

"God works in interesting ways, doesn't he?" she asked.

"Chris gave me a Bible, and I am learning about God and his ways. I need to ask you something that goes along with what you said. I don't want to bring back any bad memories or ruin this evening. I think we're in a good place now."

"Jeff, I think I can handle it. What's bothering you?" she asked.

"Mark was the attorney I went to ten years ago when I filed papers." He paused. "For divorce."

"Oh, I didn't realize he was the one. I was overwhelmed and confused at the time. I never thought about it. Where are the papers? Is that why you are here? Is this why we went to dinner?" she said with her voice shaking.

"Dinner was about us. Seeing Mark today made me realize, I never saw final papers," he said.

"What does this mean? You didn't see the papers after you filed?" she asked.

"I didn't. Remember I got that new job too. I put everything into my job and wanted to forget the pain. I might have called the firm, but I honestly don't remember," he said.

"Are we divorced? Maybe Mom has the papers or your parents. It never concerned me."

"Same here. By the way, Mark wasn't sure what happened either. Maybe we can ask your mom," he said.

"But what if?" she asked.

"What if they weren't filed?" he asked.

"Would we still be married? Isn't there a time limit?" she asked.

He shrugged his shoulders.

Robin sat in silence for a few minutes. Finally she said, "I don't know what to say. This is a shock. I trust God is going to show us what we should do."

"I'm stunned too. Running into Mark jarred my memory. Maybe it wouldn't be a bad thing," Jeff said.

The rest of the ride home was very quiet as they both thought about the fact that they might still be married.

When Betty heard the car pull into the driveway, she quietly went down the stairs. Tina and the puppy slept soundly, and she wanted to share the evening with Jeff and Robin.

Jeff and Robin hung their coats up and were staring at each other.

"Tina is so excited about that puppy. The puppy was yipping so much downstairs that we did bring the crate upstairs in her room. Did you guys have a good time?" she asked.

"Yes, we did," Robin said, and Betty noticed an odd look on Jeff's face.

"Want to watch a movie with me?" Betty asked.

Feeling guilty for leaving her with Tina and a puppy, they agreed. After changing and checking on Tina, they both came down. Betty gave them a couple of choices, and they picked *What a Girl Really Wants*, a romance. Betty observed how Jeff and Robin kept gazing at each other during the movie, but she didn't dare ask why. When the movie ended, they all just said good night and went to bed in silence.

Betty knew she needed to pray for them right away. Something had happened at dinner, but she couldn't pry.

Jeff tossed and turned. Not only did he think about dinner, but the uncertainty about the divorce papers brought other thoughts into his mind. He wondered if Robin was having difficulty sleeping too.

After almost two hours of restlessness, he turned the office light back on and reached for the Bible sitting on the nightstand. How he wished he could talk to Pastor Chris now. Reading the Bible helped him realize God was always there to talk to—24/7.

An index card with Bible verses on it on laid on the nightstand. Although he did not recognize the handwriting, he ruled out Betty, Tina, and Robin. The card read:

Matthew 6:25–34

Proverbs 3:5–6

Philippians 4:6–7

Not used to the layout of the Bible yet, he used his cell phone to look up the verses. A common theme of trusting in God and not worrying was clear in all the passages.

For ten years he had made a good living and lived very comfortably, but these past few days had shown him something in Robin he admired. Nate and Marcy supported Robin, but they each had their own lives. Robin made it all these years with Tina and trust in God. Her life had been richer than his in so many ways. Despite the circumstances—the accident, the move, the loss of her dad, and the loss of her job—she brought light to others. He envied her and wanted a faith like hers. Not for just himself, for them all. He wanted a true faith, family, and his marriage back.

Jeff got down on his knees and prayed out loud, "Lord, you know I am a new believer and I am trying to change. Thank you for these past few days. Thank you for opening my eyes to look at life the way you look at life. Teach me how to trust you. I want to. I love my family, and I want to be a family. I promise I'll do better. I'm not the same person I was two days ago or a week ago. I am worried about those papers. If I am still married, how do I tell Robin I was unfaithful? Help me."

His eyes remained closed, and he envisioned the life he wanted. He heard the bedroom door open, and he turned to see Betty.

"Sorry, Jeff. I saw the light on. Tina and I couldn't sleep either. I got her back to bed. Those verses helped me through Robin's crisis. Nate wrote them out for me, so I left them for you."

"He was a great man. How much did you hear?" Jeff asked.

Betty hesitated. "I wasn't eavesdropping, but I did overhear your prayer," she said.

"Honestly, I thought we were divorced. I didn't have any meaningful relationships, but I dated hoping to fill the emptiness. Sometimes my dates were for show, so I could get help to work up the corporate ladder."

Betty stopped him. "I'm not the one you talk to, and I don't know how to respond. Even if you and Robin don't get back together, you will still be part of Tina's life. That in itself is a whole lot better than it was a week ago," Betty said.

Jeff knew she was right. A week ago, his life had held no meaning. The video his secretary showed him changed everything.

"God is capable of doing the impossible. Your little girl has been praying about you for a long time. Look in those albums. Now, tomorrow—or should I say today—is going to be a big day. You need some sleep. Do you need tea or anything?" she asked.

"No, but thanks. I appreciate the talk and the verses. Sounds like good advice," he said.

"You're welcome," she said, closing his door.

Robin simultaneously closed her door.

God, why didn't he tell me before he took me out? Maybe he's afraid I want back child support and doesn't mean what he says. Protect my baby girl. Protect me, Lord. She laid down and stared at the ceiling until she felt the Spirit tell her, *Child, keep trusting. I will not abandon or forsake you.*

The last ten years had been nothing but complete trust in God—not in Jeff. How would she face him in the morning after what she had overheard?

CHAPTER 34

Tina and Betty were up early taking care of Blackie. He needed to go out early, and Betty helped Tina with him. She was ten, but the puppy was frisky, and Betty did not want him to run away again. Betty remembered doing the same thing with Robin all those years ago. Betty looked at the backyard and thought they might have to consider making some changes to accommodate the puppy.

Jeff's car was gone when they went out.

After a few minutes of exercise, Betty and Tina went indoors. Blackie went right to her dish of food, and Tina poured herself a bowl of cereal.

"I suppose Grandma can help out with taking care of Blackie when you go to school," Betty said.

"Help out with what?" Robin said as she entered the kitchen.

"Watching Blackie during the day when you two are gone," Betty replied.

Tina looked up in surprise.

"Blackie will be in such good hands, Tina. Don't you think?" Robin asked.

"Can Blackie go to school?" she asked.

"Honey, you know puppies don't go to school. But I promise sometimes I will pick you up with him in the car. If he behaves, that is," Robin said, pretending to be talking to Blackie.

"Say, Robin, you look like you are dressed to go somewhere. Do mind if I ask where?" Betty asked.

"Susan asked if I could stop in for a chat this morning about something. I hope it is not bad news. Tina, she asked if you would stop in too. Seems like everyone is asking about you," Robin said.

"Blackie too?" Tina asked.

"No, honey, Blackie needs to stay here. We won't be gone long. Mom, do you mind watching the puppy?" Robin asked.

"No worries. I didn't plan anything this morning. I think I will ask Jeff to pick up another crate for Blackie so we can have one up and down," Betty said. "Any other plans for today?"

"Tina, Blackie needs some shots. I am going to call the vet to make an appointment for this afternoon. Tina, do you want to go?" Robin asked.

"No," she said quickly.

"She doesn't care for shots. That is one thing that really bothers her. Do you mind if I drop Tina off after we go to Susan's?" Robin asked.

"No problem," Betty replied.

"Mom, how about I pick up some lunch today? It will be my way to repay you for watching the puppy," she said. "How about pizza and salad for us all?"

"That sounds good. Tina and I have an errand we would like to do after lunch," Betty said.

Robin was surprised, but she trusted Betty. She did wonder what kind of errand it could be, but she let it go.

"Come on, sweetie. We need to get going. Tell Blackie you will see him later. Please run up and brush your teeth," Robin said.

Tina did as she was asked.

Robin said, "I am nervous about this meeting, Mom. I hope I am not losing my job."

"Even if you were, we'll be okay. Your father has provided for us all," Betty said. "Robin, aren't you going to ask?"

"Ask what?" she said, acting like she hadn't noticed.

"Where Jeff is?"

"Did he tell you his plans for today?"

"No! I thought he told you. His car is gone."

"Don't mention anything to Tina. I don't think he would leave without saying anything to her, do you? But then again, he's done it before."

Robin's tone alarmed Betty, and she was about to ask questions when Tina came back down. Betty kissed Tina on the top of her head.

"We'll be back with the pizza and salad about twelve. Does that work Mom?"

Betty agreed. Before Robin's car pulled out, she picked up her phone. She pressed send on the message Tina had recorded for her dad.

The realization that his divorce might not be final and any relationships over the past ten years would make him unfaithful troubled Jeff. After praying and trying to sleep without success, he got up and packed his things. He was certain Robin would ask him to leave anyway. He went down the stairs quietly and felt relief when Blackie did not bark. Leaving them all behind without being honest seemed easier than hurting them with the truth. Mark sent him a text a little after eight and said he had news.

Luckily, the weather had warmed up the roads, making the shoveling around Robin's car easier. He really didn't want her to be with him when he talked to Mark about the papers and about what he'd done.

The coffee shop was busy as usual. Mark waved from the back table. He was alone this time.

"Mark, I was surprised to get your text so quickly. I thought this would take weeks. Do you want coffee?" Jeff asked.

"Actually, I do, but I've already ordered for us. Judy will bring it over when it's ready. I ordered the same thing you had yesterday. Okay?"

"Sure—and thanks. Do I dare ask what you found out?" Jeff asked.

"I am hoping this doesn't upset you," Mark said.

"Just give it to me straight," Jeff said.

"Remember I told you I took the job offer right after you came in to file those papers?" Mark said.

"Yes, I do. But didn't the firm still take care to finish the filing?" Jeff asked.

"You're not going to believe this, Jeff," Mark said.

"Try me, Mark," Jeff said.

"After I left, there was a roof leak where my office files used to be," Mark said.

"Did the water ruin them?" Jeff asked.

"No, the cleanup meant the files in the area were moved to a storage unit used for closed files until they finished. Alice, my secretary, immediately started working in the front office, which handles property cases. The new secretary's familiarity with clients took time. When I asked Alice about your file, she couldn't find any information at all. On a hunch, she went to the storage unit to look," Mark said.

"Did she find them with the closed files?" he asked.

Judy brought the coffees and set them down. "Anything else?"

"No, no thanks, Judy," Mark answered. "Jeff, I don't know how to tell you."

"Tell me what exactly?" Jeff asked.

"Your papers weren't signed by you or Robin. In the hurry to move files, your papers were placed in the old closed case files of your grandfather. We had done a lot of work for him," Mark said.

Jeff sipped his coffee and didn't speak at first. "So as my lawyer, legally what does this mean?"

"Unless you have a set of signed papers filed somewhere else, you and Robin are still married. I am so sorry that this mistake happened. Just a whole lot of different quirky things happening at once," Mark said.

"I don't blame you. I never followed up with you. I did talk to Robin about it though," Jeff said.

"What did she say?" Mark asked.

"She never thought about it," Jeff said.

"But what about other relationships? Didn't she want to marry again?" Mark asked.

"Our marriage was such a disappointment, I think she never considered dating," Jeff responded.

"You told me you thought Robin was ruining your plans for the future with the pregnancy. How do you feel about that now?" Mark asked.

"She has always been on my mind. No one could replace her in my heart. I dated, but nothing serious. I would love to stay married, but there's another problem."

"What?" Mark asked.

"I dated, and technically, I was unfaithful."

Mark empathized with his situation. "The question now is, how do we proceed? I could draw up some new papers—for free, of course. Tell me what you want," Mark said.

Jeff looked around the cafe and stared in his now-empty cup. "Until a week ago, my life was as empty as this cup. What I want is to have my wife and family. I also want a relationship with God."

Mark said, "Do you know what Robin wants? I saw you last night, and it looked like things were good between you."

"Mark, she's forgiven me for leaving. That in itself, I do not understand. We've gotten closer these past few days, but *trust* is an issue that can't be resolved overnight. It will take time. I left and never looked back. That's a huge betrayal. I didn't even help with support and now add adultery."

"My mom filled me in a little about Robin mostly. She wasn't close to Betty. Robin seems to be a strong Christian. She had good reason to be very bitter with her mom, but she isn't. Am I right?" Mark asked.

"Funny you mention that. Betty is in my corner and wants us all to be a family again. She's lost a lot of years because of pride and doesn't want Robin to make the same mistake," Jeff said.

"Well, I guess the next step is to talk to Robin. You have my number. By the way, New Year's Day is on Sunday. Will I see you all in church?" Mark asked.

"I'm not sure. I packed my things this morning," Jeff said.

"My best advice is to face Robin. Be truthful with her. If you run now, you are running from Tina too. Think about the impact on her. There would be no going back."

"Pray I don't mess up," Jeff said.

"You've got it. Okay if I pass this on to the family?" Mark asked.

"Sure. Maybe I will see you Sunday," Jeff said.

"I hope so, Jeff. By the way, you have a beautiful family. Put their needs first. Think about them," Mark said.

Jeff sat there staring at his cup, deep in thought.

CHAPTER 35

Jeff sat contemplating his conversation with Mark, wondering what to do with the information. He needed a clear answer.

"Mind if I join you?"

Jeff looked up to see Chris standing with a coffee in his hand. "What a coincidence. Actually, I thought about talking to you today. Let me get a refill. I'll be right back," said Jeff.

Chris chuckled. With God there are no coincidences. No wonder he had such an urge for a cappuccino.

Jeff came back quickly.

"Since I last saw you, my life hasn't been the same. That episode with Tina chasing the dog helped Robin move past our differences to focus on Tina," Jeff began. "After we went back to Betty's, things just kept changing. Betty let me stay with them, and we've all gotten along for a few days."

"A few days?" Chris asked.

"Yes, I took Tina to get all the dog stuff, and then we picked up the puppy. The stress wiped Robin out," Jeff said.

"Well, given the accident and the holidays, plus your appearance in town, I understand," Chris said. "That can wear anyone out."

"I enjoyed my time with Tina, and Robin is beginning to trust me again. We went out on a date last night," Jeff said.

"A date?" Chris asked.

"Yes we went to Luigi's for dinner. Betty stayed with Tina and the puppy," Jeff said.

Chris was amused. "Betty is turning the home situation around, isn't she?"

"She is, and Robin has totally forgiven her. But I ran into Mark Bailey, who happened to be an old friend in college and also the attorney I asked to file my divorce papers. Through a series of events you can't even imagine, the papers weren't filed," Jeff said.

Now Chris was laughing inside, *Lord, you're good. A series of events? Clearly you want them together.*

"So are you telling me you and Robin are still married?" he asked without letting on his thoughts.

"Robin doesn't know for sure, but I mentioned the possibility last night," Jeff said.

"How did she react?" Chris asked.

"I think shocked and confused," Jeff said. "And now ..."

"Go on," Chris said.

"I haven't been completely honest. There were no meaningful relationships since Robin, but I did have women in my life. Now I realize I was married at the time."

"That complicates things."

Over the years, Chris had heard many similar stories and had seen how God restored broken marriages and families. God was at work here, but he wanted to be careful not to give false hope.

He finally said, "Jeff, with God anything is possible. It sounds like you have repented and your heart is in the right place now. Pour your heart out to Robin, and stay in the word of God, no matter what. The Bible is the living word, which means we use it to live by. Trust God. The reality is, living in obedience will free you."

"This talk helped, but I'll admit, I'm afraid," Jeff said.

"Let's pray," Chris said.

Chris prayed over him and then said he would continue to pray.

Although Jeff felt a peace come over him during the prayer, he left the cafe without a clear decision.

Chris watched Jeff's car turn toward the highway. Running wouldn't solve anything. He bowed his head again and prayed fervently for intervention.

Robin hadn't been back to the home since the day of the concert Tina sang in. She liked the staff and the patients at the home, but being a receptionist was not what she wanted to be doing permanently.

"Tina, here we are. Momma has a meeting with Susan, so I need you to be good," Robin said.

"Okay, Momma," Tina asked.

"I'll ask about Ruth," Robin replied.

When they approached the front desk, Robin did not recognize the receptionist.

"Hi, I'm Robin, and this is Tina. I have an appointment with Susan," Robin said.

"Oh, Robin. She is expecting you. I'll call her," she said. She dialed Susan's number.

"She needs to speak with a nurse on her way and will be with you soon. It shouldn't take long," she said.

"Mind if I ask you something?" Robin asked.

"Not at all. What can I help you with?" she asked.

"When did you start working here? And what's your name?" Robin asked.

"I'm Alice, Mary's niece. I came home for Christmas, and Aunt Mary asked if I could fill in for a few weeks," Alice said.

Robin was relieved and also felt guilty for not trusting God.

"Robin, Tina, hi. I've missed you guys. Come on in. Tina, Mary wondered if you would mind visiting with Ruth. She keeps asking about you," Susan said.

"She was going to ask you if she could. Those two got a little attached," Robin said.

Mary appeared in the lobby to greet them. "Tina, Ruth is so happy you're here." They headed off toward the dementia wing.

"Robin, first thing I wanted to ask, how are you feeling?" Susan asked.

"I'm almost fully recovered. The holidays are always draining, and then Tina's dad showed up," Robin said.

"If you don't mind me asking, how is that working out for you?" Susan asked.

"Better than I thought. He actually helped me a lot this week, especially on Monday when Tina went missing," Robin answered.

"My staff helped with the search. I'm glad things ended well. I asked you here for a different reason though," Susan said.

Robin waited anxiously.

"Don't look so worried. Tina's little sing-along made a huge impact on our residents. I'm aware of your prior work at the developmentally disabled facility, and this job wasn't the one you were hoping for," Susan said.

"Go on," Robin said. She wasn't sure where this conversation was going.

"The holidays are not the only difficult times for the residents. Statistics show about eighty-five percent of residents in this type of facility don't get visitors after the first six months. Most residents realize they will never leave this home," Susan said.

"Eighty-five?" Robin asked.

"Unfortunately, that's an accurate number. When Tina came to sing, the residents responded favorably. Your Tina melted the heart of a particularly difficult man, and he responded with tears of joy. It triggered a happy memory for him," she said.

"I was watching Ruth and didn't notice. I worried about how they'd respond," Robin said.

"Ruth was amazing when she played the piano. We've been concerned about her depression. We talked about it at a staff meeting, and we changed her medications. Ruth was misdiagnosed with dementia and

AS ANGELS SING

is now being correctly treated for a thyroid issue. In fact, her family is coming to take her home," Susan said.

"Tina helped?" Robin asked.

"You saw Ruth's change after she met Tina. I went to our regional director about what happened. We brainstormed ideas and discussed options for a section of this facility not being used. We let a doctor rent it out for a while, but he suddenly retired. I have a proposal for you," Susan said.

"A proposal?" she asked

"We would like you to consider helping us start a day care for children under the age of five. Also, we want an after-school program. We want it in this building because with your expert knowledge we thought you could coordinate more activities between the elderly side and the small children. What do you think?" Susan asked.

"So tell me more about what that would look like," Robin asked.

"Robin, you make the decisions. We trust you. You came to us with very strong credentials that make you perfect for this job. Take a look at this budget proposal and decide if you're interested. I think you'll note a substantial pay raise too," Susan said, handing her a folder.

Robin opened the folder, and her eyes couldn't believe her salary. "Really?"

"Yes. Robin, I knew your situation when you started the receptionist job. Marcy called. But you did your job with such integrity despite being overqualified for it. You've inspired and impressed everyone here. This area needs affordable day care. Many people are out of work and take jobs with less pay like you did," Susan said.

"I agree. When do you need an answer?" Robin asked.

"After the first of the year, say by January 5. If you decide you don't want it, your old job is waiting," Susan added.

"This is just so incredible. Thank you for this offer. I thought I was losing my job," Robin said.

"Not a chance. Like I said, we are pleased. Even though Tina will not be in the day care, we still want her to sing for the residents. Promise me that," Susan said.

"I'm sure Tina will agree. She loves coming here," Robin said.

"Speaking of Tina, I think I hear Mary outside with her," she said.

Susan opened the door and Tina was waiting with Mary.

"I hope to see you both in church soon," Susan said.

"New Year's Day falls on Sunday, and we're looking forward to starting a new year with worshipping God," Robin said.

They said their goodbyes, and Robin glanced up at the sky when they went out the doors. *Thank you, Lord. Thank you for providing faithfully. Please give me wisdom with Jeff. I don't know what to do.*

CHAPTER 36

Robin and Tina came home with pizza and salad in hand. Tina's arrival was a welcome sight for Betty and Blackie.

They gave Tina a few minutes to play with the puppy before they put him in the crate.

"So how did things go?" Betty asked.

"We need to talk," Robin said.

Robin told Betty about Susan's offer.

"Mom, I'm taking the puppy to the vet after lunch. Are you okay with being with Tina?" Robin asked.

"Actually, I wanted to take Tina to the movies this afternoon. She wanted to see that new animated movie. Right, sweetie?" Betty said.

"Yes," Tina said even though she wanted to play with her puppy.

Betty was becoming much better at reading Robin's mood, but she could tell she wasn't sharing something.

"Robin, we are going with Kristen and the kids, so we will probably stop by their house for a visit afterward. Unless you want us to come home?" Betty asked.

The rest of lunch consisted of Tina's news about Ruth and the other residents. She finished her lunch and then played with the puppy.

Robin and Betty cleaned up.

"Everything all right?" Betty asked.

"Susan's news was great—a better job than a receptionist. I want to know if Jeff and I are really divorced or not. I went upstairs, and his things are gone," Robin said.

"You know the car was gone this morning. Where did he go?" Betty asked.

"Maybe he's running again."

"Robin, things will work out the way God plans them," Betty asked.

"I trust him in everything. Look at us. I am so grateful to have you back in my life, Mom. I overheard your conversation with Jeff last night," Robin said.

"Jeff needs to talk to you about his concerns and issues," Betty said.

"We do need to talk. I felt such anger hearing about his past that I almost stormed in to tell him to leave. I don't want Tina to think I made him go though. Another part of me reminds me that faith is about forgiving like God did. Love is unconditional. I think of Joseph in the Bible and what his brothers did to him. He forgave them all," Robin said.

"You're going to have to find him before he does leave town. Only you can decide if you want him to go."

"It's not about just me. Tina needs Jeff, and if I'm truthful—I do too," Robin said.

"Robin, Jeff is still very much in love with you," Betty said.

"I still love him. I never stopped, but he obviously was unfaithful," she said.

"Can you forgive him?"

"The thought of him with someone else hurts. I couldn't sleep last night with the anticipation of Susan's meeting and finding out about my marriage. I searched the Bible for answers."

"What did you find?"

"God extended mercy, love, grace, and compassion over and over. He forgives. If I don't forgive, I won't be forgiven."

"Maybe that's the answer," Betty said. She went over and hugged her. Robin sobbed quietly in her arms.

Jeff parked his car near the exit to the interstate. Leaving wasn't as easy as it had been ten years ago. Thoughts of Tina and Robin went through his mind. He reached in his pocket and took out his cell phone. Who would he call?

A voice message awaited his response. He pressed play to listen and expected a message from his secretary. Instead Tina had left a message saying, "I love you. Momma loves you. Miss you, and Blackie does too."

"I love you both—more than words can say," he said out loud.

Then he started the car and turned back to Lima.

CHAPTER 37

Robin put Blackie in the crate and drove to the vet's. Her mind kept reliving the dinner and what Jeff had said to her mom. Was he running? Did he find out they were still married and leave? She needed answers.

The appointment didn't take long, and Robin was glad Tina didn't see the shots. The vet assured Robin that Blackie was a healthy puppy. He hated shots as much as Tina did. Robin put the puppy in the crate in the backseat and glanced across the street. Jeff stood by his parked car watching her. He walked across the street to her car.

"I wondered where you'd gone today. I thought you probably left town," she said.

"Actually, I started to. I met with Mark, and because of series of mistakes, our divorce didn't go through. We're legally still married. Mind if I come to the house to talk?"

"Mom and Tina are at the movies. Follow me home."

Jeff followed her to the house. He carried the puppy crate, and Robin unlocked the door. She was feeling quite anxious to finish the conversation.

"So you were leaving because we are still married and you don't want to be?"

"Robin, you deserve a better man than me. I'm ashamed to admit I've had casual, meaningless relationships over these ten years. I didn't know about the papers."

"If you had known, would that have made a difference?"

"Absolutely. I made many mistakes, but I took our wedding vows seriously. Robin, I love you. I love Tina and every minute of this past week. I'm sorry this hurts you. Tell me what you're thinking."

"Jeff, part of being a Christian is forgiving and extending grace to others like God does to us. Every day I sin; I try not to, but I do. The Bible is full of people who made huge mistakes, including marital issues. My favorite love story is Hosea. He forgave his unfaithful wife several times. Read it. I want to believe in us again."

"Robin, then all things are possible with God? Right?" Jeff said.

"How can this work? I can't move out from here. Mom and I missed ten years. Tina loves it here and has adjusted to a new life. Susan just offered me a great new job," Robin said.

"A new job?" he asked.

"Yes, my dream job. I haven't agreed. I want to think about it, but I'm sure I want it," Robin said.

"You should take it," Jeff said.

"What about your job?" Robin asked.

"I am the CEO. I own a lot of stock and can change my job description if I want. Robin, I don't care about any of that. I want to trust God the way you do. It will work out as long as you love me and forgive me," Jeff said.

"I do, and I love this. We've been a family. I love it," she said.

"Then, we stay married?" he asked.

"We stay married," Robin said.

"There is just one more thing to do," Jeff said.

"What's that?" she asked.

Jeff went over to her and took her in his arms. Robin let herself give him a kiss filled with as much passion as he was giving.

Betty and Tina stood on the porch steps watching.

"Praise God," Tina shouted

Betty and Tina came into the house, making a lot of noise and making sure they didn't shock them. Robin's face was red, and Jeff stood smiling. Tina went up to Robin and gave her a hug and then hugged Jeff.

"We had a great time at the movies. The theater was packed, but what a great movie," Betty said. "What shall we do for dinner?"

"I'm making dinner tonight, Betty. I will be back in about twenty minutes while I run to the store. Go relax," Jeff said.

Tina and Betty took Blackie into the family room.

Robin waited in the kitchen until he returned with steaks and baked potatoes. As Jeff scrubbed the potatoes, Robin asked, "Jeff, do you think we should tell them?"

"Depends on what you'll be telling them," he said.

"We are back together. Am I right?" Robin said.

"You're right. Back together as husband and wife," Jeff said.

"Jeff, this feels so right. We were good together. This time will be even better," Robin said.

"Better how?" Jeff asked.

"God is with us. I want us both to have a strong faith together. I want to be committed together. Is that something you can do?" Robin asked.

"Chris and Kristen gave me a Bible. I will admit I am new at this. I believe God was with us when we searched for Tina. Look what he's done with us, with Betty. I'm in, Robin. I want a faith like yours," Jeff said.

"I've waited a long time for this. It will take some getting used to. Hold me please," Robin said.

Jeff came over and held her for quite a few minutes. They didn't say anything.

"I think I better finish dinner up. The potatoes are almost done, and I need to broil the steaks. Want to help?" he asked.

"Love to," Robin said.

Tina was peeking through the kitchen doorway.

"Poppy, I miss you. Thank you, Jesus," she whispered.

A little while later Jeff went in the family room and called Betty and Tina.

Jeff had cooked a great steak dinner. Before they started to eat, he asked if he could say a blessing.

He said, "Lord, thank you for my beautiful family. We love you, Lord, and thank you for our many blessings. Bless this food we are about to eat. Thank you for giving my family back to me. Thank you for my wife, Robin. She is a blessing just like Betty and Tina. Help us make our plans for the future. Amen."

"Does that mean you're still ..." Betty paused, being careful not to say too much.

"Yes, the divorce was never completed due to complicated circumstances. We are still legally married, and we want to be. I love him, Mom," Robin said with happy tears running down her face.

"Tina, I'm going to be living with you guys. A lot is changing, Betty, and I don't want you to worry. You won't be alone. We will figure things out and don't need to do it all tonight," Jeff said.

"I'm so happy," Betty said.

"Tina, did you hear that? Daddy is home to stay," Robin said.

Tina smiled. They wondered if she already knew somehow.

They ate the delicious dinner Jeff cooked and talked about their future.

"Susan's new job won't change my hours but will change my pay. I'm going to look the agreement over carefully before I sign anything, but I trust Susan," Robin said.

"Quite the day!" Betty said.

"Robin, you might want Mark to look it over. He is in town for a few more days."

"Good idea," Robin said. "Mom, I forgot tomorrow is New Year's Eve. I volunteered to serve lunch at the homeless center because I wasn't able to do it on Christmas Day."

"Me too," Tina said.

"Make that three," Betty said.

"I would love to serve again, but I do need to do a few things tomorrow. I really need to talk to my parents, and I have a few people to see. I will stop in though," Jeff said.

They all pitched in and cleaned up the kitchen.

Blackie needed to go out, so Jeff and Tina got the leash and took him out.

"Robin, now that you and Jeff are back together, will he still be staying in the office? Don't answer unless you want to," Betty said.

"Mom, ten years waiting for him to come back to me is long enough. I have missed him, and I am not wasting any more time," Robin said.

"Great answer. I will go up and add a few pillows. I can take some clothes out of the closet. Do I need to move anything else?" Betty asked.

"It doesn't need to be done tonight, Mom. He isn't going to change his mind. God answered Tina's and Dad's prayers and worked everything out in his own timing," Robin said.

"I guess he did," Betty said. *I wonder if they will have more children.* She smiled to herself.

CHAPTER 38

Jeff dialed his parents when they all left for the homeless center. Luckily, his mom answered.

"Mom, hi. Hope I'm not interrupting. How are you?" Jeff asked.

"I'm fine. Where are you? We've been worried," his mom said.

"I'm still in New York. I'm with Robin," Jeff said.

"Robin? Is everything okay?" she asked.

"Mom, can you put Dad on the extension phone please?" Jeff asked.

"Sure," she said. In a few minutes, he heard a click.

"Morning, son. This sounds urgent. Are you okay?" his father asked.

"Mom and Dad, something incredible has happened in my life. It is a long story with circumstances too difficult to explain over the phone. I don't have much time. Robin and I are still married," Jeff said.

His mom let out a gasp. "Mom, this is a good thing. Robin and I found our way back to each other. We still love each other," Jeff said.

"Son, I am so happy for you," his father said.

"There is more, much more. Robin did not abort the baby ten years ago. She is alive and well. Her name is Tina," Jeff said.

"But we thought …" His mom stopped before finishing.

"You thought the baby had Down syndrome. She does, and she is still a remarkable little girl. So, Mom and Dad, you have another granddaughter," Jeff finished.

"Oh, Matt, another granddaughter. How wonderful!" his mom said. "Jeff, I hope you are committed to support them. How did Robin manage all those years?"

"We knew Robin was incredible when I married her. I'll let her tell you the story. Is it possible for you to fly in to Rochester and drive down to Lima for Sunday morning service at ten thirty?" Jeff asked.

"Is there a particular reason?" Helen asked.

"I am going to try to renew our wedding vows during the service tomorrow," Jeff said.

"Son, we will check and do our best. Let us get back to you," his dad said.

"This is great news. These last years we've felt so distant from you. You really haven't been the same, son," his mother said.

"Part of me was missing. I also want you to know, I found a new faith in God. Robin is such a fine example. I can't wait to see you. Now I need to make some other arrangements or this won't happen," Jeff said.

"We will talk to you soon, son," his father said and hung up.

Next, Jeff called Marcy and filled her in on his plans. He asked if she could be at the church also. Marcy agreed. He continued with a call to Mark. Mark and Cathy were all so happy for the news. Robin already had sent a text saying they were back together. Cathy liked the fact that they would renew their vows on New Year's Day.

Jeff had sent Chris a text and asked if they could meet at the church. Chris had to stop by the church anyway. He just hoped Jeff had made the right decision.

Chris pulled in the driveway ahead of Jeff.

"Hey, Jeff. It sounded urgent—are you okay?" Chris asked.

"Things are good, but I need your help," Jeff said.

Relief filled Chris. He loved seeing broken families mended. With the Christmas season not officially over until the Epiphany, the season of miracles was not over.

When they got settled in his office, Jeff's excitement could not be contained any longer.

"Chris, Robin and I both want to stay married," Jeff said.

AS ANGELS SING

Chris was relieved. "What happens with your job and her job?" he asked.

"I will let Robin tell you about her new job offer. We'll be staying here," Jeff said. "My job will change as far as location. I do a great deal of work online with video conferencing. I'll travel some, but I have a bunch of new ideas in my head. I'm thinking we might be able to open a branch here."

Chris thought, *Lord, you are doing a mighty work here. New branch, new jobs, just what this community needs. Thank you!*

"Jeff, this is welcome news. Sounds like a new beginning in all areas of your life," Chris said.

"That is why I am here. Robin and I married about twelve years ago. We started dating in college and married after graduation. Robin's pregnancy came a little over a year after we married."

"So you weren't together for long," Chris said.

"Not married long, but our dating and early marriage were great. Robin, Tina, Betty, and everyone forgave me. The slate is clean, and we're all going to work together to figure out what is best for us," Jeff said.

"I am glad you are including Betty. Widows often end of being alone. She's finding her faith again too," Chris said.

"You're right. Betty has been very supportive. I promise, I have no intention of abandoning my family again. My job became my marriage. I didn't come here to talk about that, though, and I would like to get some counseling soon," Jeff said.

"That's good to hear. This will be a transition period, and I can help with that," Chris said.

"I came here to ask if it is possible for Robin and me to exchange wedding vows tomorrow during the service," Jeff said.

Chris smiled and thought, *A new year, new beginnings. This will be perfect.*

"I'm flexible, and the congregation would approve. Any special requests? Does Robin know you want to do this?" Chris asked.

"No, and I don't want her to. I would like it to be a surprise, unless you think that is a bad idea?" Jeff asked.

"What a beautiful surprise. You say you are back together. Does that mean living together?" Chris asked.

"Yes, but we are taking things slowly. I want this ceremony to recommit myself to her in front of everyone so she doesn't doubt my sincerity. I'm also making the vows to God. Last time I broke the better and worse part," Jeff said.

"Actually, I think this is a great idea. Do you mind if I let Kristen in on this?" Chris asked.

"Sure, she's been such a help to me. I've asked my parents to fly in, plus Marcy and Mark agreed to stand up for us. I want Tina to stand with us, and I want to commit to her too," Jeff said.

"You have thought this out. Don't worry, this will be a pleasure," Chris said.

"Then we'll see you tomorrow," Jeff said.

"Tomorrow," Chris said.

CHAPTER 39

The homeless center was bustling as was usual the during the winter months. With the recent layoffs and inclement weather, people spent as much time as possible at the center.

When Jeff entered, he saw Robin and Betty behind the counter serving lunch. Tina was out in the dining room singing for patrons. In between she would pour water and talk to them about her new puppy. Jeff looked around, half expecting Blackie to be with the patrons. Betty waved to him and pointed over to Tina.

"She's daddy's little girl," one of the other workers said to Robin.

Robin liked the sound of that. She noticed Jeff in the distance hugging Tina. They interacted so naturally. Last night had been wonderful and felt so natural between them too. They were taking things slow.

"Robin, I would like to go to the grocery store on the way home. Tina can come with me if you don't mind. She wants me to make something special for New Year's Day lunch. Why don't you and Jeff have lunch at Charlie's?" Betty said.

"Charlie's—I love their flatbread. I haven't been there in months. Are you sure?" Robin asked.

"I'm sure, and you don't need to ask," Betty said, laughing.

"Sorry, Mom. I never want to impose," Robin said.

"I have missed ten years. I am making up for it," Betty replied.

"Thanks, Mom. Jeff and I do need to talk more about our jobs," Robin said.

"Honey, he's changed so much. I can't wait to witness his Christian growth," Betty said.

"Me too. He is such a new believer, so hungry for God's word. The more he reads the Bible, God will help him understand how many great figures in the Bible were redeemed. Then he will understand why we forgave him," Robin said.

"God is a God of second chances, that's for sure," Betty said.

"We'll be home in a few hours, Mom," Robin said, taking her apron off. "Pete, I'll look at my schedule and try to find more ways to help after I figure out my next few weeks."

"Me too," said Jeff. "I want to be a regular here as well."

Pete grinned. "The more help I get, the more I can do. Thanks."

"Jeff, how about going to Charlie's for a bite? This might be our last bit of quiet before the reality of work hits us. I want to talk to you about that, okay?" Robin asked.

"Sounds great," Jeff said.

Chris took a look at the bulletin for the next day. The New Year's service usually consisted of singing Christmas hymns. He would have to give Marilyn a call. Kristen would know how to make the sanctuary look special.

He dialed Marilyn's number. "Marilyn, I'm sorry to call you at home. Jeff Anderson and Robin reconciled and want to renew their wedding vows during the service tomorrow. Who can we get to play music?" he asked.

"Chris, remember, Ruth Henderson is home now. Since they have adjusted her medication, she's fine. She would be glad to play whatever you want, I'm sure. Remember, Tina helped snap her out of the depression. She would love to do it," Marilyn said.

"That's a good idea. Can you think of anything else?" Chris asked.

"Actually, yes. Let me call a few people to pray all goes well, and of course, we need refreshments afterward. Don't you think?" she asked.

"Yes. We Presbyterians like to eat. Thanks," Chris said.

"And Chris, I just thought about the envelope Nate left with you. He said if Robin and Jeff got back together, you were to open it," she said.

"I'll find it. Thanks for reminding me. I wonder if he knew this day would come."

"Chris, he was a faithful member of the church even though Betty didn't come. With his powerful faith, I'm sure he never doubted they would find their way back to each other," Marilyn said.

"With a little help from above. Thanks, Marilyn. Please be sure Susan is made aware, but remember when you talk to anyone, this is a surprise for Robin, Tina, and Betty," he said.

"See you tomorrow," she said and hung up.

Next he dialed Kristen and told her the news. She was happy for them and wanted to put together some extra flowers and decorations.

Ruth was living at her daughter's house now and was more than happy to do what he asked.

Now that he had a few minutes, he found the envelope from Nate. The envelope contained a music CD. Chris put it in his player and was surprised by the contents.

Nate had a wedding message for Robin, Jeff, and Tina. Then he sang the song "You Raise Me Up." Nate stopped singing in the choir when Betty stopped coming to church. He had such a beautiful voice, and this song was perfect to go with his message.

Chris couldn't wait for the service tomorrow. The congregation had really pulled together this season, and things were turning around.

Chris looked forward to pursuing his own dreams for future missions. Even pastors needed to be reminded of the hope we all have in Jesus, and this year was a testimony to God's faithfulness. Chris reminded himself that God is who he says he is and also does what he promises in his word. This Christmas season certainly had brought the same hope that came so many years ago in a manger. Tomorrow would be perfect for a recommitting for everyone.

CHAPTER 40

Jeff and Robin enjoyed their lunch together.

"So do you think you'll take the job?" Jeff asked.

"Yes, I think I will. Since my field is counseling with a secondary degree in childhood education, this will be exciting," Robin said.

"Then it's all set for you. My job is mostly done with video conferencing, so I am hoping Betty will let me use the office as my office," he said.

"The office was Dad's. Remember, he traveled, and he worked from home once a week. Mom has her own room upstairs for scrapbooking and sewing," Robin said. "Besides, we don't need to decide everything right away. Let's enjoy today."

He took her hand. "I love you, Robin Anderson, and I love spending time with you."

During lunch they talked about how next week's the routine would be different. They would need to help Betty out with Blackie. Jeff would help out when he worked at home. The crate helped because Blackie wasn't an overly active now. Seemed like all he needed was love too.

New Year's Eve consisted of a quiet family evening at home again. Betty made her famous meatloaf, and they sat around doing a puzzle.

When it was close to midnight, Betty went in the kitchen to a closet. She brought back a box with party hats and blowers.

"Sorry, but this is my first New Year's with my family. We are all going to wear one of these and celebrate," Betty said.

She poured some sparkling cider in glasses, and they turned on the TV to watch the countdown.

Jeff gave Robin a big kiss, and Tina and Betty giggled.

"To new beginnings and a great new year for us all," Jeff said, holding his sparkling cider.

They all toasted and felt the bond between them.

Jeff got up early despite having stayed up talking with Robin. He made sure the coffee was ready and got some pancake batter mixed. Tina loved her pancakes, and they didn't have much time to get ready.

"My, look at you at work in the kitchen," Betty said.

"Betty, I'm looking forward to going to church today. I think I'll wear a tie," Jeff said.

"You don't need to wear one," Betty said.

"Yes, I do. Would you mind encouraging Tina and Robin to maybe wear dresses? Tell them you're not sure what the tradition is today at the church or something like that," Jeff said.

"Jeff, you're up to something, aren't you?" Betty asked.

"Starting the year right, and I do have something planned at church," he said and winked.

"Okay, I'll leave you to your fun. I'll be right back," Betty said.

Jeff finished cooking breakfast and called them all down. Robin and Tina were wearing dresses. Jeff couldn't help but admire them.

"You both look beautiful! I'm looking forward to our first time going to church together. Now, Tina, let me put this napkin on so you don't ruin that pretty dress," Jeff said.

"Are those pumpkin pancakes?" Robin asked.

"Tina's favorite," Jeff said back to her.

Betty joined them, and they said grace together. Robin was happy grace was a habit. They finished and went upstairs to brush their teeth.

At ten, they all got in Robin's car.

Pulling into the parking lot, Robin said, "Boy, attendance sure is up. It was better on Christmas Eve, but I thought today would be different."

They got out of the car, and Mark came up to them. "Hi! Glad to see you guys. Mind if we sit with you?"

"Sure, that would be great," Jeff said.

When they entered the church, Robin's eyes got bigger. Jeff's parents stood waiting.

"Surprise," said Helen. "Robin, we couldn't be happier for you both. Is this our granddaughter?"

"Yes, this is Tina. Tina, this Grandma Helen and Grandpa Matt," Robin said. She watched them embrace, and Tina gave them each a hug.

"Glad you are here. I guess we will be sharing this little one now," Betty said.

"Shall we find a seat down front?" Jeff said.

They all walked in as a group. The front row had special flowers marking it, and flowers sat in a box in the front row.

"Jeff, what is going on?" Robin asked.

"I thought for New Year's we could renew our vows, or should I say, I want to make a new commitment to my family. Is that okay?" Jeff asked.

Robin was stunned but pleased. She looked at Betty, Matt, and Helen so happy to see each other. So many lives were affected by their marriage.

Marcy walked up. "Well, friend. Are you ready for this?"

"I am. It is hard to believe this all is happening," Robin said.

"It is. Just be happy. You so deserve it," Marcy said.

The piano music starting was their cue to sit. Robin noticed that Ruth was playing, and she smiled. Tina was trying to control herself, and she gave a small wave.

Chris went up to the pulpit. "Today is the first day of our new year. Every year we talk about new beginnings and trying to improve in some area. My message today will be about beginnings, and we have a family here starting with a fresh commitment to each other. I'm sure you all know the Andersons."

The service started and was a routine service until after the sermon. Chris asked Robin, Tina, Jeff, Mark, and Marcy to come up.

He started, "God had a plan when he designed marriage. It is the bringing together of two people in love and commitment. This family committed to each other years ago but today would like to reaffirm their vows. The difference today is a child will be part of the commitment. You three hold hands, please."

They held hands and repeated what Chris asked them to. He even had special words for Tina to say. Everyone looked on with wonder and delight.

Each one responded, "I do" after Chris's words.

Kristen, Marilyn, Molly, Ruth, Susan, and all the other members were choked up as the family stood there.

Jeff and Robin kissed, and the congregation clapped.

"Now, Mr. and Mrs. Anderson, there's a special surprise for you. If you could all please take a seat," Chris said.

They all sat in the front row.

"As you all know, Nate Johnson left us a few months ago, and we all miss him. His spirit is still here. He left a special CD to be played at his daughter's renewing of her wedding vows. It is my honor to play it for you all now," Chris said, and he went back to his seat behind the pulpit.

Molly turned on the sound system and played the message to Jeff and Robin. Then Nate sang "You Raise Me Up." There wasn't a dry eye in the church.

As Chris closed the service, he announced, "In the Presbyterian tradition, there will be a reception for the Anderson family in the fellowship hall. You're all welcome to attend."

Robin took Jeff's hand. "Thank you for doing all this. It means so much to me. I am looking forward to having a lifetime with you and our family. With God, we won't go wrong."

"I believe that, and I believe what Chris said. What God has joined together, let no one take apart. I love you!"

"I love you too. Let's go get some food. I can't wait to catch up with your mom and dad. Where's Tina?" Robin asked.

"Mom, Dad, and Betty have her. Let them spoil her a little," he said.

"Maybe just a little," she said, laughing.

ABOUT THE AUTHOR

Linda is a retired teacher with years of classroom experience inspiring students to write from the heart. As Angels Sing is her first break out novel and is dedicated to her sister Tina who had Down syndrome. The main character exhibits Tina's loving spirit. Linda supports agencies that support pro-life, adoption and the Christian faith.

Lightning Source UK Ltd.
Milton Keynes UK
UKOW04f1431211017
311402UK00001B/48/P

9 781512 786972